"Would you be willing to marry me now?"

James asked her.

Summer stared at him, but no words came out.

"Summer, have I utterly shocked you?"

"Yes," she admitted in a high squeaky voice.

James smiled at her. "I'll admit, this is the first impulsive thought I've entertained in years."

Summer knew she was going to cry, but these were happy tears, because she loved him so much. "James, we'd be doing the right thing, wouldn't we?"

He didn't hesitate. "Yes. It's what we both want."

"You love me?" He'd never said the words, not once.

His look softened. "Very much."

"Everyone is going to think we're crazy."

James grinned broadly. "Probably."

Dear Reader,

Welcome to Silhouette **Special Edition**...welcome to romance.

Bestselling author Debbie Macomber gets February off to an exciting start with her title for THAT SPECIAL WOMAN! An unforgettable New Year's Eve encounter isn't enough for one couple...and a year later they decide to marry in *Same Time, Next Year*. Don't miss this extraspecial love story!

At the center of Celeste Hamilton's *A Family Home* beats the heart of true love waiting to be discovered. Adam Cutler's son knows that he's found the perfect mom in Lainey Bates—now it's up to his dad to realize it. Then it's back to Glenwood for another of Susan Mallery's HOMETOWN HEARTBREAKERS. Bad boy Austin Lucas tempts his way into the heart of bashful Rebecca Chambers. Find out if he makes an honest woman of her in *Marriage on Demand*. Trisha Alexander has you wondering who *The Real Elizabeth Hollister* is as a woman searches for her true identity—and finds love like she's never known.

Two authors join the **Special Edition** family this month. Veteran Silhouette Romance author Brittany Young brings us the adorable efforts of two young, intrepid matchmakers in *Jenni Finds a Father*. Finally, when old lovers once again cross paths, not even a secret will keep them apart in Kaitlyn Gorton's *Hearth, Home and Hope*.

Look for more excitement, emotion and romance in the coming months from Silhouette **Special Edition.** We hope you enjoy these stories!

Sincerely,

Tara Gavin
Senior Editor

Please address questions and book requests to:
Silhouette Reader Service
U.S.: 3010 Walden Ave., P.O. Box 1325, Buffalo, NY 14269
Canadian: P.O. Box 609, Fort Erie, Ont. L2A 5X3

DEBBIE MACOMBER

SAME TIME, NEXT YEAR

SPECIAL EDITION®

Published by Silhouette Books
America's Publisher of Contemporary Romance

To Beth Huizenga,
my friend.
I admire your strength,
your romantic heart
and your love of life.

 SILHOUETTE BOOKS

ISBN 0-373-09937-1

SAME TIME, NEXT YEAR

Copyright © 1995 by Debbie Macomber

This edition published by arrangement with Harlequin Enterprises B.V.

® and TM are trademarks of Harlequin Enterprises B.V., used under
license. Trademarks indicated with ® are registered in the United States
Patent and Trademark Office, the Canadian Trade Marks Office and in
other countries.

Printed in U.S.A.

Books by Debbie Macomber

DEBBIE MACOMBER

hails from the state of Washington. As a busy wife and mother of four, she strives to keep her family healthy and happy. As the prolific author of dozens of best-selling romance novels, she strives to keep her readers happy with each new book she writes.

Prologue

New Year's Eve—Las Vegas, Nevada

James had been warned. Ryan Kilpatrick, a long-time friend and fellow attorney, had advised him to stay clear of the downtown area on this night. The crowd that gathered on Fremont Street between Main and Las Vegas Boulevard was said to be close to twenty thousand.

James hadn't been able to resist. Although he had a perfectly good view of the festivities from his hotel-room window, he found the enthusiasm of the milling assembly contagious. For reasons he didn't care to examine, he wanted to be part of all this craziness.

The noise level on the street was earsplitting. Everyone seemed to be shouting at once. The fireworks display wasn't scheduled to begin for another thirty minutes, and James couldn't imagine there was room for a single other soul.

A large number of law-enforcement officers roamed the area, confiscating beer bottles and handing out paper cups. A series of discordant blasts from two-foot-long horns caused James to cringe. Many of the participants donned decorative head wear handed out by the casinos and blew paper noisemakers that ceremoniously uncurled with each whistle.

James remained on the outskirts of the throng, silently enjoying himself despite the noise and confusion. If he were younger, he might have let his hair down and joined in the festivities himself.

Thirty-six wasn't old, he reminded himself, but he looked and felt closer to forty. Partners in prestigious law firms didn't don dunce caps and blow colorful noisemakers. This wasn't James's scene. Generally he was much too stodgy and staid for such nonsense, but it was New Year's Eve and staying inside his hotel held little appeal.

Impatient for the fireworks display, the crowd started chanting. James couldn't make out the words, but he understood the gist of the message. It amused him that the New Year's celebration took place three hours early in order to coordinate with the one taking place in Times Square in New York. Apparently no one seemed to care about the time difference.

As if in response to the demand, a rocket shot into the air from the roof of the Plaza Hotel. The night sky brightened as a star-burst exploded and spilled light across a black satin night. The crowd cheered wildly.

Although he intended to stand on the sidelines, James found himself unwillingly thrust deeper and deeper into the crowd. Luckily he wasn't prone to claustrophobia. People crushed him from all sides. In another time and place he might have objected, but the joy of the celebration overrode any real complaint.

It was then that he saw her.

She was struggling to move away from the crowd, with little or no success. James wasn't sure what it was about her that had originally attracted his attention, but his gaze found her and stayed. Joyous shouts and cheers rose like steam over a boiling kettle in the tightly packed congregation. The young woman didn't share the excitement. She looked very much as if she'd rather be any place in the world than where she was.

She was a fragile thing, petite and delicate looking. Like a salmon battling to swim upstream, she fought against the crowd but found herself trapped despite her best efforts.

James didn't intentionally make his way toward her, but soon found himself gravitating in her direction. Within a matter of minutes she was pressed up against his chest, her chin tucked in her neck in an effort to avoid eye contact.

"Excuse me," he said.

She glanced up at him and attempted a smile. "I was the one who butted into you."

He was struck by how beautiful she was. Her soft brown hair curved gently at her shoulders, and he swore he'd never viewed eyes more dark or soulful. He was mesmerized by her eyes, by the deep pain he read in their depths.

"Are you all right?" he felt obliged to ask.

She nodded and bit into her bottom lip. He realized how pale she was and feared she was about to faint.

"Let me help." He wasn't a knight in shining armor who rescued damsels in distress. Life was filled with enough difficulties without his taking on another's troubles. Yet he couldn't resist helping her.

She answered him with a quick but proud nod of her head.

"Let's get out of here," he suggested.

"I've been trying to do exactly that for the last twenty minutes." Her voice was thin and tight with pain.

James wasn't sure he could do any better, but he felt obliged to try. Taking her by the hand, he scooted around a couple passionately kissing, past a group of teens with dueling horns, the discordant sound piercing the night. Others appeared more concerned with catching the ashes raining down from the fireworks display than where they stood or who they bumped against.

Perhaps it was his age or the fact he sounded authoritarian, but James managed to maneuver them through the crush of humanity. Once they were off Fremont Street, the crowd thinned considerably.

James led her to a small park with a gazebo that afforded them limited privacy. She sank onto the bench seat as if her legs had suddenly given out from under her. He realized she was trembling and sat next to her, hoping his presence would offer her some small solace.

The fireworks burst to life overhead.

"Thank you," she whispered. She stood, teetered, then abruptly sat back down.

"You want to talk about it?" he asked.

"Not really." Having said that, she promptly burst into tears. Covering her face with both her hands, she gently rocked back and forth, her soft mewling wails clawed at his heart.

Not knowing what to do, James wrapped his arms around her and gently held her against him. She felt warm and soft in his embrace.

"I feel like such a fool," she said between sobs. "How could I have been so stupid?"

"We're often blind to what we don't wish to see."

"Yes, but... Oh, I should have known. I should have guessed there was someone else. Everything makes sense now...I couldn't have been more blind."

"Perhaps," he conceded.

She straightened and James handed her his pressed handkerchief. She unfolded it, wiped away the tears and then clenched the kerchief in both hands, holding it in her lap.

"I'm sorry," she choked out in a strangled voice.

"Talking it out might help," he suggested.

She took several moments to mull this over. "I found him with another woman," she said tightly. "He wanted me to come to Vegas with him after Christmas, and I couldn't get time off from work. I was the one who insisted he go and have fun with his friends. Then ... then I was able to leave early this afternoon and I wanted to surprise him on New Year's Eve...so I drove straight here. I surprised him, all right."

And got the shock of her life, as well, James mused.

"I found them in bed together." Her words were barely audible as if the pain were so intense she found it difficult to speak. "I ran away and he came after me and...and tried to explain. He's been seeing her for some time...he didn't mean to fall in love with her, or so he claims." She laughed and hiccuped simultaneously, the sound echoing pitifully in the night.

"You were engaged?" he asked, noting the solitary diamond on her left hand.

She nodded, and her gaze fell to her ring finger. As if remembering the diamond for the first time, she jerked it off and stuffed it in her purse. "Jason had seemed distant in the last few months, but we've both been terribly busy with the holidays. I noticed he didn't seem overly disappointed when I couldn't get time off from work. Now I know why."

It was probably better that she learned of Jason's penchant for a roving eye before they were married, but James didn't offer platitudes. He hadn't wanted to hear them himself.

"The thing is I really love him." She shook almost uncontrollably. "I want to claw his eyes out, and yet I know I'll always love him."

"Are you hoping to patch things up?"

Her head snapped up. "No. It's over. I told him that and I meant it. I could never trust him again, but you know what?" She hesitated and drew in a deep, wobbly breath. "I think he was grateful when I broke the engagement. He doesn't want me back—he wants *her*." She stiffened and locked her shoulders as if bracing herself against an attack.

"It hurts terribly right now, but it'll get better in time," James said, and squeezed her hand.

"No, it won't," she whispered. "It will never get better. I know it won't."

James partially agreed with her. A portion of his heart would always belong to Christy Manning. Even now he had trouble remembering her married name. She wasn't Christy Manning any longer, but Christy

Franklin, and her husband was the sheriff of Custer County, Montana.

"It'll take a year," James said, wanting to assure her that the pain lessened with time.

"Not with me. I'll never get over Jason."

"You believe that right now, because the pain's so fierce you can't imagine it ever going away, but it does, I promise you."

Slowly she turned to study him. "You know?"

He nodded. "Five years ago the woman I loved broke off our engagement." He laughed a little derisively. "You see, there was this small problem. She fell in love and married someone else while engaged to me."

"That's terrible," she said with a sigh of righteous indignation. "What kind of woman would do that?"

"It's not as bad as it sounds. You see, her parents are good friends of mine, and I realize now they pressured Christy into accepting my engagement ring. She was fond of me and agreed because she wanted to make her family happy. I don't think she ever realized how much I loved her."

"Do you still love her?"

It might have been a kindness to lie, but James found he couldn't. "Yes, but not in the same way."

"Despite what I know, I can't imagine myself not loving Jason." She straightened and wiped the tears from her cheeks, which glowed softly in the moonlight. "I suppose I should introduce myself since I've cried all over your shoulder. I'm Summer Lawton."

"James Wilkens."

The two exchanged brief handshakes. Summer lowered her gaze. "I wish I could believe you."

"Believe me?"

"That it'll take a year to get over Jason. It doesn't seem possible. You see, we've been dating for nearly five years and have been engaged for the past six months. My whole life revolved around him."

At one time James's life had revolved around Christy.

"We were apart for less than a week," Summer continued, "and I was so lonely, I practically went through contortions to get to Vegas just so we could be together for tonight."

"The first three months are the most difficult," he told her, remembering the weeks following the breakup with Christy. "Keep busy. The worst thing for you to do is stay at home and mope, although that's exactly what you'll want to do."

"You don't understand," she insisted. "I really love Jason."

"I really love Christy."

"It's different for a man," she argued.

"Is it really?" he countered. "A year," he reiterated. "It'll take a year, but by then you'll have worked through the pain."

Her look revealed her doubt.

"You don't believe me?"

"I just don't think it's possible. Not for me. You see, I'm not the type who falls in love at the drop of a hat. I gave everything I had to give to Jason. It's like my whole world caved in and there's nothing left to live for."

"Shall we test my theory?" he asked.

"Test your theory?"

"Yes. Meet me back here on New Year's Eve, one year from tonight."

"Here? In this gazebo?"

"That's right," he said. "Right here."

"Same time, same place, next year."

"Same time, same place, next year," he echoed.

Chapter One

Summer picked up the mail on the way into her apartment and quickly shuffled through the usual bills and sales flyers. The envelope was there, just as it had been the first of the month for the past eleven months. A letter from James.

He hadn't a clue how much she looked forward to hearing from him. The first letter had come shortly after they'd met that fateful New Year's Eve and had been little more than a polite inquiry. She hadn't written him back mainly because she was embarrassed over the way she'd spilled out her heart to a complete stranger.

His second letter had arrived the first of February. He told her about the first month after his breakup with Christy, how the pain intensified when he'd expected it to lessen. His honesty and generosity had touched her heart. She found it uncanny the way her own anguish mirrored his. She wrote back then, just a short note to tell him how she was doing, to thank him for writing.

That was how it had all started. James would write the first of every month and she'd answer. Gradually their letters grew in length, but never beyond the one quick monthly exchange.

In the year since Summer had met James Wilkens, she'd been tempted to phone him only once. That was the day Jason married. Ironically his wife wasn't the cupcake he'd brought to Las Vegas, but someone he'd recently met. Summer had felt wretched and had holed herself up in her apartment with a quart of gourmet ice cream and three rented videos. She'd made it through the day with a little fudge swirl, and a whole lot of grit.

Holding James's latest missive in her hand, Summer tore open the envelope and started reading on her way into the apartment.

"The letter's from your lawyer friend, isn't it?" Julie, her roommate, asked. Wearing shorts and halter top, Julie traipsed barefoot through the apartment, munching on a carrot.

Summer nodded, kicked off her shoes and lowered herself onto the padded wicker chair. Her eyes never wavered from the page.

"He wants to remind me of our agreement," Summer said, pleased he hadn't forgotten.

"Agreement?"

"To meet him in Vegas on New Year's Eve."

"Are you going?"

Summer had never seriously considered not following through with the promise, although she probably should have thought twice about meeting a stranger.

But she knew James, was comfortable with him. He was harmless, like a favorite uncle.

"Are you going?" Julie repeated.

"I'll be there."

"What's James like?" Julie asked, sitting across from Summer. The two had been friends all through high school, and Summer had been especially grateful for Julie's unwavering friendship in the past year.

"He's older," Summer said, chewing on the corner of her mouth in an effort to remember all she could about him. "I'd guess he's at least forty and a bit of a stuffed shirt. He's about six feet tall and he must work out in a gym or something because I remember being surprised by how muscular and strong he was."

"Is he handsome?"

Summer had to smile. "To tell you the truth, I don't remember."

"You don't remember?" Julie was incredulous. "I know you were upset and everything, but surely you noticed."

"He has brown hair and beautiful brown eyes." She raised her hand to her hair and wove a strand around her finger. "And there's a bit of silver in his sideburns that gives him a debonair look. As I recall, he's more distinguished looking than handsome."

"You certainly devour his letters. One would think there was something romantic going on between the two of you."

Summer did care for James, but not in the romantic sense. He'd helped her through the most difficult night of her life. Not only had she clung to him and cried on his shoulder, but he'd also stayed with her until the early hours of the morning, listening to her pain, comforting and reassuring her.

"We have a lot in common" was all she'd say to Julie's comment about a romance developing between them.

"I have a feeling about the two of you," Julie said, and her forehead creased with a thoughtful frown. "I think you're falling in love."

Love. Not Summer. She'd decided last New Year's Eve that she was finished with love. It sounded melodramatic and a bit ridiculous to be so confident she'd never love again, but she had come by that conclusion the minute she found Jason with his girlfriend. Her feelings hadn't changed in the past eleven months.

Although he'd never said as much, she was certain James felt the same way after losing Christy. It'd been six years, and from what she knew about him there wasn't a significant other in his life even now. There wouldn't be in hers, either.

This didn't mean that Summer never intended to date again. She'd gotten back into that scene almost immediately. Pride had prompted her actions in the beginning. Later she wanted to be able to write James and tell him she was back into the swing of things. He'd applauded her efforts and recounted his own endeavors in that area soon after Christy had broken off the engagement. As she read the account of his antics, she'd laughed, truly laughed, for the first time in months.

"You're going to meet James on New Year's Eve, and everything will change," Julie said with a knowing smile.

"What do you mean everything will change?"

"You won't view him as a distinguished older man with a kind heart any longer," Julie prophesied. "You might be surprised to discover he's more man than you suspect.''

''Julie, I told you he's got to be forty years old.''

''You're sure of this?''

''No,'' she admitted reluctantly. ''But... I don't know. I picture James sitting in front of a stone fireplace, smoking a pipe with his faithful dog sprawled out on a rug at his side.''

''An Irish setter, no doubt.''

''No doubt,'' Summer agreed with a soft laugh. James was wonderful—she had no argument about that—but she could never see herself falling for him. Nor would he be interested in someone like her. The man was a distinguished attorney, while she starred in a musical version of *Beauty and the Beast* at Disneyland. Working in the theater wasn't an easy way of making a living, but Summer loved the challenge and the excitement.

''You might be surprised,'' Julie said with a soft, lilting voice that suggested she expected great things to happen for her friend this New Year's Eve.

Summer freely admitted she was nervous about the rendezvous with James. She arrived at the gazebo nearly fifteen minutes early and was surprised to find him already there. He was sitting on the bench, the same one they'd shared a year earlier. In that moment Summer had a chance to study the attorney with fresh eyes.

The first thing that struck her was that Julie was right.

He was nothing like she remembered. Dignified and proper to the very back of his teeth, but he was without a doubt the most compelling male she'd ever seen.

She recalled Julie's inquisitiveness, wanting to know if James was handsome. If Summer were to answer the question now, she'd give an unequivocal *yes*. But he wasn't handsome in the traditional sense. He certainly wasn't beachboy-calendar material or even someone who'd be asked to pose for *Gentleman's Quarterly*. James Wilkens was devastatingly appealing in a way that spoke to her heart. This was a man of conscience, a man of integrity, a man of honor. All at once Summer felt as if the oxygen had left her lungs.

He saw her then and slowly stood. "Summer?" He sounded equally surprised. His eyes widened briefly as if he was unsure it was really her.

"Hello, James. I'm early," she said, feeling guilty at being caught staring at him so blatantly. "I'm always early...it's a family trait."

"I am, too," he admitted.

Summer had been looking forward to this evening for weeks. There was so much she wanted to say, so much she had to tell him. All at once she couldn't think of a thing to say. "The streets are crazy," she said in a hurried effort to make conversation. "I didn't want to take a chance of being late."

"Me, either," he said. "I hope you don't mind, but I made dinner reservations."

"I don't mind in the least." She stepped into the gazebo and sat down next to him.

"So," he said, as if he wasn't sure where to start. "How are you?"

Summer laughed lightly. "A whole lot better than I was last year at this time. I told you Jason married, didn't I?"

"You wrote about that."

Summer rarely felt shy, but she did now. She owed James more than she could possibly repay. "Your letters were a godsend," she said, not knowing where to start, "especially the first few months. I don't know what I would have done without you."

"You would have done just fine." How confident he sounded, as if there was never a doubt that she'd recover from Jason's betrayal.

"I owe you so much," she said, wanting to let him know that he'd made a difference and how grateful she was. "The first of every month, I'd race to the mailbox, knowing I'd hear from you. Your letters helped more than I can say."

"I enjoyed your letters, as well," he admitted. Fireworks splashed across the night sky, momentarily diverting their attention. "Do you want to join in the festivities?" he asked.

Summer shook her head. "Do you mind?"

He smiled. "Actually I'm just as glad. The crowd got to be a bit much last year."

"I'm so glad you were there," Summer said fervently, her heart spilling over with gratitude. "You were like a guardian angel God sent to help me that night."

"You helped me, too."

"Me? But how?" Summer could hardly believe that.

"It's true," James assured her. "Seeing your pain so fresh and potent reminded me of how far I'd come in the years since losing Christy."

"Was it especially bad knowing she'd married her sheriff friend?" Summer asked tentatively. The worst of it for her had been when she'd learned Jason had married. Friends, under the guise of being kind, were more than happy to relate the details of his wedding and what they knew about his bride. Every tidbit of information had cut like a knife.

"Yes."

James wasn't a man to mince words, she noted. "Weren't you angry?" In like circumstances, Summer knew she would be. How anyone could treat James in such a shabby manner was beyond her. To be engaged to a man as wonderful as James and then to secretly marry someone else was the most underhanded thing Summer had ever heard.

"I wasn't angry at first," he admitted thoughtfully. "That came later and was responsible for me taking up squash. I worked out my aggression on the court. It helped."

Summer knew that was a game similar to racquetball. A sport an attorney would enjoy, she decided.

"It was hard knowing Jason had married, wasn't it?"

She lowered her gaze and nodded. "Other than the first few weeks after he broke the engagement, the day of his wedding was the worst. It seemed so completely unfair that he should be happy when I was hurting so terribly. If it was ever in me to hate him, it would have been then."

"And now?"

"Now," she repeated, mulling over his question. "I certainly don't hate Jason, but I don't love him in the same intense way that I did a year ago. He was a big part of my life, and my world felt empty without him."

"Does it feel empty now?"

She didn't need time to know the answer to that. "Not in the least. I'm happy, James, and I didn't think that would ever be possible again."

"Then I was right. It took you a year."

She laughed and nodded. "I'm over him and happy to be with you tonight."

"There isn't anyone I'd rather be with on New Year's Eve." He glanced at his watch and stood. "I hope you haven't eaten."

"I didn't. I only arrived a little over an hour ago, and I'm starved." She'd been anxious about their meeting, so her appetite had been nil all day. Her stomach wanted to make up for lost time now.

James led her into the Four Queens Hotel, weaving his way between the crowds gathered around slot machines and gaming tables. With several thousand people milling around outside, she'd assumed the casinos would be less crowded, but she was wrong.

James took her hand then, gripping it firmly in his own. Summer was surprised how good it felt to be linked to him. By the time they walked down the stairs leading to Hugo's Cellar, a world-class restaurant, Summer felt as if she'd survived a riot. So much for all the time she'd taken with her appearance. She felt fortunate to be in one piece.

After a short five-minute wait, they were escorted to a booth and presented with elaborate menus. The room was dimly lit, and candles flickered gently, casting dancing shadows about the restaurant. The noise and bustle from upstairs and on the streets outside the casino were blessedly missing.

They dined in leisure, shared a bottle of white wine and a calorie-rich dessert. It amazed her that they had so much to talk about. James asked her about her job at Disneyland, and seemed genuinely interested in her budding career as an actress.

When she learned he'd recently been appointed as a superior court judge to the King County bench, she insisted on ordering champagne to celebrate.

"You should have told me much sooner," she chastised.

"It's only temporary," James explained, looking uncomfortable now that he was the focus of their conversation. "I've been appointed to serve out the term of Judge Killmar, who was forced to retire for medical reasons."

Summer wasn't entirely sure he would have told her if she hadn't asked him about his own hopes and dreams. Only then did he mention it was a lifetime goal to serve as a superior court judge some day.

"But you intend on running for the position yourself later, don't you?"

"Yes," he admitted reluctantly. "But the primary isn't until September, and the election's in November. There're no guarantees."

"You'll win," Summer insisted with supreme confidence. And wagging her finger at him, she added, "And don't give me that look. I can't imagine anyone not voting for you."

James's eyes met hers. "You're good for my ego," he said, and then added under his breath, "too good."

By the time they finished with dinner, it was well after eleven. As they made their way out of the casino, someone handed Summer a speckled foil crown and a noisemaker. She donned the hat and handed James the whistle.

Summer had long since lost track of the time, but guessed that the New Year was fast approaching. It seemed impossible that her night with James was nearly over. She didn't want it to be.

The streets had thinned out considerably following the fireworks display. They were standing on the sidewalk outside of the Golden Nugget when a cheer rose from inside the casinos.

"It must be midnight," James commented, and ceremoniously blew the noisemaker. "Happy New Year, Summer," he said in a voice so low it was almost a whisper.

"Happy New Year, James."

They stood facing each other, and then, as if this were the moment they'd patiently anticipated all evening, they slowly moved toward each other. Summer noticed how James's eyes darkened as her own fluttered closed. She wanted this. Needed this.

She sighed audibly as his mouth settled over hers.

Chapter Two

Summer was no novice when it came to kissing, but James left her breathless and clinging to him for support. She hadn't anticipated anything like this happening. What she'd expected was for them to lightly brush their lips together and then laugh and wish each other a happy New Year.

It hadn't happened like that.

The instant James's mouth was on hers, she had gone languid. Their tongues had met and engaged in erotic games that left her weak and trembling.

The shock of her reaction left her immobile with her arms locked around his neck and her body pressed intimately to his, her lips seeking more, wanting more.

Summer would have liked James to kiss her again and again. She wasn't sure what was happening between them; all she knew was that she didn't want it to

end. Only she wasn't sure how to ask him to continue
or if she should.

Slowly, with what she thought might be reluctance,
he released her. She stood there looking at him, her
arms dangling stiffly at her sides while her face red-
dened with acute embarrassment. She thought to tell
him her usual response to a man wasn't this blatant.

"Happy New Year," James said in a voice that
didn't sound anything like himself. He cleared his
throat and inserted a finger inside his stiffly starched
collar and eased it around his neck.

"Happy New Year," she whispered, and stepped
away from him.

James reached for her hand and clasped it firmly in
his own. Summer was grateful for his touch. They
started walking, with no destination in mind, at least
none that Summer could remember. Her mind
whirled, and she looked at James, wondering if he felt
as confused and uncertain as she did. Apparently he
did because he grew quiet and introspective.

"I believe I'll call it a night," James announced
unexpectedly. He checked his watch and frowned.
Summer suspected it had been a year since he'd last
stayed up past midnight. He was so prim and proper,
so serious and sober. Yet she'd enjoyed every minute
of her evening with him. They'd talked and laughed,
or at least she'd laughed. James had smiled, and she
had the impression he didn't do that often, either.
Every time he'd grinned, Summer had felt rewarded.

Now she'd ruined everything. She couldn't bear to
know what he thought of her. An apology, words of
explanation stumbled over themselves in her mind, but
she couldn't make herself say any of them, simply because she wasn't sorry for the kiss. Yes, it had gotten

involved, but she'd savored it, relished it and hoped he had, as well.

"I'll probably call it a night, too," Summer said. She waited, hoping he'd suggest they meet some time the following day. He didn't.

By the time they reached the Four Queens, where they were both booked for the week, Summer was miserable.

"James," she said as they walked across the lobby. Either she apologized now or regret saying nothing. "I'm sorry. I...don't know what came over me. I don't generally...I can only guess what you must think of me and..."

"You?" He hesitated in front of the elevator. "I was wondering what you thought of me. I can only ask your indulgence."

The security guard asked to see their room keys before calling for the elevator. James easily produced his while Summer shifted through the contents of her oversize purse before being able to supply evidence of her own.

The elevator arrived, and they both stepped inside. Still James didn't ask to see her again. Summer's heart grew heavier as they ascended. Her room was on the tenth floor, and his was on the fifteenth.

The silence closed in on them like a too-tight belt. The elevator stopped at her floor. The large doors swooshed open, and James stepped aside.

Summer glanced toward him expectantly. Apparently he didn't intend to see her again. It made sense really. A superior court judge wouldn't be interested in dating an actress.

"Good night," she said brightly as she stepped out of the car.

"Good night, Summer," James said softly.

She hesitated, hoping he'd ask her at the last moment, but he didn't. Discouraged, Summer returned to her room, unlocked the door and walked inside. She sat on the edge of the mattress to process her muddled thoughts.

When Summer had requested a week's vacation, she hadn't intended on spending every available minute with James. She knew he'd taken several days himself, and he'd probably been thinking the same thing.

Summer slipped off her shoes and wiggled her nylon-covered toes against the thick carpet. If it wasn't so late, she'd call Julie and admit to her friend that she was right. One evening with James, and she saw him in a completely different light. The moment she'd viewed him in the gazebo that evening, she dismissed the father-figure image she'd set in her mind all these months. The kiss convinced her James was more than a friend than she realized. What became of their relationship depended on several things, the most important of which was James himself.

The phone by the nightstand rang, and Summer hurriedly groped for it.

"Summer, I'm sorry to bother you."

Her heart gave a sigh of relief. "Hello, James."

"I've got a rental car," he said. "I know it's probably not something you'd generally consider fun, but I was thinking I'd drive over to Hoover Dam in the morning. Would you care to join me?"

"Why wouldn't I consider that fun?" she asked.

"I'm sure there are friends here your own age you'd prefer to spend your time with and . . ."

"Friends? I thought you were my friend."

"Yes, but I was thinking friends closer to your own age."

His answer irritated her. "I'm not exactly sure what you're insinuating, but if it is what I think it is, you're wrong, James."

"Listen, Summer, all I want to know is if you'd like to join me in the morning."

That may have been his original question, but she wasn't nearly finished with what she had to say. "I took a week's vacation, and I know you have several days, as well. I don't expect you to entertain me or keep me company, if that's what you're worried about, because I can find plenty to do on my own."

"I see."

"And yes, there are any number of people my age in Vegas. There would be in any city. If you want my company, fine, but if you'd rather not see me again, I can accept that, too." Not easily, but she'd do it and have a perfectly wonderful week without him.

The line was strangely silent.

"James? Are you still there?"

"Yes. Are you always this direct?" he asked after an awkward moment.

"No, but I didn't want there to be any misunderstanding between us. I value your friendship, and I don't want it ruined because of something silly."

"Nor do I." A short pause followed. "Forgive me for being dense, but I'm not sure I understood your answer. Are you going to Hoover Dam with me or not?"

Summer had waited all evening for this invitation, and having him say the words was almost anticlimactic. "Would you like me to come?"

"Attorneys do this all the time, you know," he said with a chuckle.

"Do what?"

"Answer a question with one of their own. Yes, Summer, I'd very much enjoy your company."

"Great. When do you want to leave in the morning?"

James told her, and they set a time to meet in the lobby the following day. Summer replaced the receiver and lay back on the bed, tucking her hands beneath her head. She smiled softly to herself, anxious for the morning.

James hadn't thought of himself as necessarily old, seeing that at thirty-six he was the youngest superior court judge serving on the bench. Being with Summer, however, made him feel downright ancient.

She was adequately named. Being with her was like walking along Green Lake in the middle of August when the air carried the scent of blooming flowers and sunshine warmed the afternoon. Spending time with Summer was akin to magically capturing a moonbeam and being granted the gift of holding it in the palm of one's hand.

James couldn't remember any one time when he'd smiled more than during their dinner together. She told him about playing her role at Disneyland. Her joy and enthusiasm for her job spilled over like bubbles in a champagne glass. He could have listened to her all night.

She wasn't content to do all the talking, however, and to his surprise he found himself telling her about the ins and outs of his own position on the court and the upcoming election, which was vital to his career.

His life was very different from her own. While Summer worked in the delightful world of fantasy, he struggled with the often cruel, unjust world of reality.

Naturally he couldn't give her any details of the cases he'd heard, but just talking about his short time on the bench had lifted his spirits considerably. It felt good to share his thoughts with her, and she made him feel as if what he had to say was worthwhile and important.

Then they'd kissed. Talk about sexual chemistry! For the life of him, James couldn't explain what happened when she'd come into his arms. He certainly never intended the kiss to become that involved, but once he started, nothing could have stopped him.

He feared his reaction had shocked Summer, but apparently that wasn't the case. Later she'd apologized to him for her reaction, and James hadn't known what to say. She seemed to think she'd done something wrong. She hadn't. The truth was, she'd done everything right. He was the one who was at a loss to account for his own behavior.

James sat down in the lobby and waited for Summer. He was eager for this outing. He'd decided earlier not to invite her, feeling it would be unfair to dominate her time. She was young and beautiful, and he sincerely doubted that she wanted to spend her vacation with a stuffed shirt like him.

He'd gone to his hotel room and congratulated himself on not mentioning the trip to Hoover Dam. Ten minutes later he'd talked himself into calling her on the off chance she might be interested.

Well, she'd certainly told him. A smile courted the edges of his mouth. Summer had seemed downright angry with him when he suggested she'd prefer to be with friends her own age.

Frankly James liked the idea of being her friend. The operative word being *friend*. He wasn't going to kiss her again—that was for sure.

First off he was afraid of a repeat performance of what had happened in the street when they'd wished each other a happy New Year. Secondly he was light-years too old for her. He tremendously enjoyed her company, but then any man would. Summer was a delight. He wasn't going to ruin the strong bond they shared by allowing the two of them to become romantically involved.

Summer stepped off the elevator, and James watched as every eye in the place seemed to gravitate toward her. She was stunning. It wasn't the clothes she wore, although the pretty pink pants and matching sweater flattered her. It was Summer herself. She beamed.

Her gaze searched the lobby until she found him, and then she smiled. James felt as if he were a knight of old being honored by his queen.

He stood and waited for her to join him. "Did you have breakfast?" he asked.

She nodded. "Hours ago."

"Me, too."

"If you're ready, we can be on our way." All he had to do now was stop staring at her. James had experienced the same phenomenon when he'd first seen the Hope diamond in the Smithsonian Institute in Washington, D.C., several years earlier. Summer was a rare and precious jewel, and he struggled within himself not to make a complete and utter fool of himself in front of her.

The valet took his ticket for the rental car, and they waited for the college-age youth to drive the large luxury sedan to the back of the hotel.

When the car arrived, the young man opened the car door and helped Summer inside. James was almost jealous to have been denied the privilege.

They traveled in a companionable silence out of Las Vegas. James had carefully studied the map so he knew which freeway to take.

"Do you ever think about her?" Summer asked.

For the life of him, James didn't know whom she was talking about. "Who?"

She laughed and the sound was musical. "That's answer enough. Christy. At least I think that was her name."

"Ah yes, Christy." James mulled over Summer's question. "Sometimes. Generally when I'm feeling especially lonely or when I see a pretty little girl with pigtails. It's times like those that I wonder what Christy's and my children would have looked like."

"How long has it been now?"

"Six years."

"Six years," she repeated, and stared out the side window.

"Do you still think about Jason?" he asked.

She lifted one shoulder in a halfhearted shrug. "Sometimes. It's different with me, though."

"Different?"

"From what you told me about Christy, she went to Montana to help her sister and met someone there."

"She would have broken the engagement right away, but it seemed like a heartless thing to do over the phone." Even now James was eager to defend her. In some unexplainable way he felt good about that.

"When she did get back, her mother, who'd badly broken her leg, had arranged for a huge engagement party and I was heavily involved in an important lawsuit. I never blamed Christy for not telling me about Cody right away. She had her reasons."

"I blame her," Summer said stiffly. "It was a rotten thing to do."

"You blame Jason, too, don't you?" This was who their conversation was really about, James suspected. Something had happened recently that had hurt her all over again.

"Right before I left," she said in a small voice, "a friend called to tell me Jason and his wife are expecting a baby."

"A friend?" James wondered about that. There seemed to be a certain type of individual who delighted in being the first to deliver bad news.

"I'm going to be twenty-eight next month," she confessed.

"From the way you said that, one would think you're going to apply for your retirement benefits."

Summer smiled. "I suppose I sound ridiculous."

"No, you sound hurt. It's only natural, but that pain will fade in time, as well, especially if you meet someone else and become involved in another relationship."

"You didn't."

James had no argument. "It wasn't because I'd dedicated myself to loving Christy the rest of my life. To be fair, I'm not entirely sure I know why I never became involved again. I never made the decision not to."

"Do you date?"

"Occasionally." Recently two women had made it plain that they would more than welcome his attention. James was flattered and he did enjoy a night out now and again, but he could never seem to garner much enthusiasm for either woman. Frankly he feared if he revealed more than a little interest, he'd find himself married with a ring through his nose. Both were politically ambitious, and when it came to a wife, James had another type of female in mind.

"What about you?" he asked, then mentally kicked himself for asking. The answer was obvious. Someone like Summer had a long line of men waiting to date her.

"I don't date all that often," Summer surprised him by saying. "It's funny, when Jason first broke up with me I saw a different man every night. Within a month I was sick of it, sick of pretending I didn't care, sick of telling everyone about all the fun I was having."

"And now?"

"I haven't been out all month. December is crazy anyway with Christmas and family obligations and everything else. November...I went to a dinner party with a member of the cast, but it was as friends, and it was more a favor to Steve than anything else."

Silly as it seemed, James was offended that she didn't count their dinner the night before as a date. He certainly had. Their time together had been the highlight of the year for him.

"My parents want me married," she murmured thoughtfully. "They hinted at it a number of times over Christmas."

Now that was something James could identify with himself. "My father's been hounding me for years to marry, but his real interest lies in grandchildren."

"I'm not willing to marry just anyone."

"I feel the same way."

They glanced at each other and then quickly looked away as if they'd said something that would embarrass the other. Silence filled the car. James didn't know what Summer was thinking, but he knew where his thoughts were taking him and it spelled trouble.

As they neared the outskirts of Boulder City, James thought to mention some of the information he'd read. "This is the only city in Nevada that doesn't allow gambling."

"Boulder City?"

"The city was built for the men who worked on the construction of the dam. I don't know the reason why, but I'd guess it has something to do with the fear the workers would squander their hard-earned cash on the gaming tables. If that were to happen, their families would see none of it."

"I wonder if it helped," Summer mused aloud.

The next hour and a half was spent driving to and over Hoover Dam. They didn't stop for the tour. The day was windy, and James was afraid Summer's sweater wouldn't be enough protection against the cold.

Once they were back on the Nevada side, they stopped long enough to take pictures. The wind blew against James as he snapped several scenic photos of the dam.

Far more of his shots were aimed at Summer. She was a natural ham and struck a variety of poses for him. He wanted a keepsake of his time with the beautiful young actress.

James asked another tourist to get a picture of the two of them together. He placed his arm around her shoulder and smiled into the camera.

"Can I have a copy after they're developed?" she surprised him by asking, rubbing her hands up and down her arms in an effort to warm herself.

"Of course," James agreed, pleased that she'd asked.

He turned up the heater when they returned to the car. He noticed that Summer's eyes drooped closed about ten miles outside of Boulder City. He located a classical-music station on the radio, and the soft strains of Mozart lulled her to sleep.

She woke when they were on the Las Vegas freeway. Startled, she sat up and looked around. "Wow, I must be stimulating company," she said, and smiled.

"I'm accustomed to the quiet, don't worry about it."

"James," she said, and yawned. She placed her hand in front of her mouth and waited a moment. "What do you think of women who ask men out on dates?"

"What do I think?" he repeated her question, never having given the subject much thought. "Well, I can't rightly say since it's never happened to me."

"Do you view them as aggressive?"

"Not necessarily. From what I understand, having the woman invite the man out is a common practice these days. Times have changed."

She smiled, and her eyes fairly danced with excitement. "I'm pleased to hear you say so because I bought two tickets to a magic show this morning. I'd enjoy it very much if you went with me."

James had certainly walked into that one with his eyes wide open. "A magic show," he repeated. Actually he was more than pleased. He hadn't even dropped her off at the hotel and already he was looking for an excuse to see her again.

"It's the late show, as it happens, which doesn't start until eleven. You'll come with me, won't you?"

"I'd be more than pleased." If he wasn't driving a car, James would have danced a jig.

After spending nearly the entire day with James, Summer counted the hours until they met for the magic show. She was dressing when the phone rang.

"Hello," she said, thinking it could only be James. Her heart gladdened at the thought.

"Summer, it's Julie."

"Julie." Summer had attempted to call her friend a number of times, but had gotten sidetracked with one thing and then another. She was pleased to hear from her roommate.

"You sound surprised to hear from me."

"I am."

"I couldn't stand it any longer. How's it going with you and the distinguished attorney?"

Summer sank onto the edge of the mattress. "Really well. By the way, he's a superior court judge now."

"That's great, so you're getting along really well," her friend echoed in knowing tones. "Do you still see him as a father figure?"

"No way," Summer said, and laughed. "There's only eight years between us."

"So," her friend's voice dipped, "tell me what's been happening."

"Well." Summer wasn't sure where to start, then decided to plunge right in. "He kissed me, and Julie, it was incredible. I don't ever remember feeling anything this powerfully sensual in my life."

"So there's electricity between the two of you?"

That was putting it mildly. Hoover Dam should produce that much electricity. "You could put it that way."

"This is just great."

"We drove out to see Hoover Dam this morning, and tonight we're going to a magic show."

"This sounds promising."

It felt that way to Summer, as well. "James invited me to drive out to Red Rock Canyon with him tomorrow and feed the burros."

"Are you?"

"Of course." It had never occurred to Summer to refuse. She didn't care if he asked her to study goat dung; she would have gladly traipsed along just for the opportunity to be with him.

"Julie . . ."

"Yeah?"

"Would you laugh at me if I told you I was falling in love with this guy?"

"Nope. I've seen it coming for months. You pored over his letters as if they were written on Mt. Sinai. For days after one arrived, it was James this and James that. I'm not the least bit surprised. This guy must really be something."

Summer's heart sank as she confronted the facts. "He's a judge, Julie. A superior court judge. I'm an actress. We're too different. Oh, it's fine here in Vegas, but once we leave, everything will go back the way it was before."

"You don't want that?"

"No," Summer admitted after some hesitation.

"Then you need to ask yourself exactly what it is you do want," Julie said.

Her roommate's words rang in her mind all through the magician's performance. Summer sat next to James and was far more aware of him than the talented performer on stage. There was magic in the air, all right. It sizzled and sparked and all but ignited. But it didn't have a thing to do with what was happening on stage.

After the show, James escorted her to his car. They were parked in a lot outside the casino. The luxury sedan was tucked away into the shadows.

"You've been quiet this evening," James commented after he helped her inside the car.

"I talked to my roommate this evening," she told him when he slid into the driver's seat next to her.

"Does it have something to do with Jason?"

"No," she answered, and shook her head for emphasis. James inserted the key to start the car. She placed her hand on his forearm to stop him. "James," she said softly, "I know this is an unusual request, and I'm sorry to make a pest of myself, but would you mind very much kissing me again?"

His Adam's apple moved up and down his throat. "I don't think it's a good idea."

"Why not?"

"In light of what happened the first time we kissed, it seems unnecessarily risky."

"I see," she murmured, disappointed.

"Summer, listen," he said as though he were at the end of his patience. "You're beautiful and very sweet, but I'm far too old for you."

"If you're looking for an excuse, James Wilkens, then you're going to need something stronger than that." This was the second time he'd brought up their age difference, and it made her good and mad. "Forget I asked," she said heatedly. "It was a stupid idea."

"That's exactly what I said." He turned the ignition switch, and the engine fired to life.

"You're probably going to tell me you didn't feel anything, either. Go ahead and lie, but we both know that's exactly what it is—a bold-faced lie."

James expelled a labored sigh. "I said nothing of the sort."

"Then you're afraid?"

Summer noticed the way his hands tightened around the steering wheel. Even in the faint light of the moon, she could see how white his knuckles were.

"I prefer to think of myself as cautious."

"Naturally," she mumbled.

What surprised Summer was how much this rejection hurt. No doubt James viewed her as immature and naive. Pushy, as well. She was probably the first woman who had ever asked him out on a date and certainly the only one who had ever sought a kiss.

Shame circled hot color in her ears. The sooner they were back to the hotel and she could escape the better.

The engine revved, but they didn't seem to be going anywhere. In fact, James had pulled the car onto the side of the road.

"You might as well know," James muttered, and turned off the car. "I've had one hell of a time keeping my hands off you as it is. It doesn't help matters that you're asking me to kiss you."

Having said that, he turned her into his arms. His lips were hungry and hard, his kiss long and deep. He broke it off abruptly, his chest heaving.

"There," he murmured, "are you satisfied now?"

"No," she whispered, and directed his mouth back to hers.

This time the kiss was slow and sweet. Long and deeply involved. Her mouth nibbled his, and she was amazed, utterly and completely amazed, by how good it was.

"Summer," he whispered, "we're going to have to stop."

"Why?" she asked, and her tongue outlined his lips.

James groaned, and Summer experienced an intense sense of power.

"I don't have a lot of control when it comes to you," he admitted brokenly.

"I don't mind."

"I wish you hadn't said that." He kissed her again, deeply, using his tongue to breach the barrier of her lips and explore the inside of her mouth. Her own tongue shyly met his with soft, welcoming touches.

By the time the kiss ended, Summer was clinging to James, mindless of anything but what was happening between the two of them.

His hand moved slowly across her stomach and upward to close over her breast. Her nipples burned and throbbed, and a sigh mingled with a groan.

"Summer...for the love of heaven, we're in a car."

"I know."

James braced his forehead against her, his breathing hard and uneven. After he gained some semblance of control, he locked his arms around her and drew her tight against him. For the longest time all he did was hold her.

It felt like heaven to be in James's arms. Summer felt both cherished and protected.

"I was afraid something like this would happen," he murmured.

"Something like what?"

He groaned. "Summer, think about it, would you?"

"I am thinking about it, and if you're referring to touching my breasts, well, I'm glad you did. I like it when you kiss me and touch me. I assumed you liked it, too."

"I do," he whispered, "that's the problem."

"If you claim you're too old for me, I won't be held responsible for what I say or do."

He chuckled at that. "All right," he said, and brushed the hair away from her face. "I'm not too old for you in years, but in attitude."

"Well that's easy enough to change. We'll start first thing in the morning."

"Start what?" he asked, clearly confused.

She kissed him, letting her lips play over his. "You'll see."

Chapter Three

James was waiting in the lobby for Summer bright and early the following morning. Her face broke into a disgruntled look when she saw him. With her hands braced against her hips, she walked a complete circle around him.

"What?" he asked, thinking he might have left part of his shirttail showing.

"Where did you say we were headed?" she asked.

He had a sinking suspicion she already knew the answer. "Red Rock Canyon."

"Do you always wear a shirt and tie to feed wild burros?"

James wore a shirt and tie to everything. "Yes," he answered.

"That's what I thought. Then I'd like to suggest that we stop off at a mall first."

"The mall? Whatever for?"

She looked at him as if she would like to have his intelligence questioned. "I'm taking you shopping," she announced. "If you have any objections, you'd better voice them now."

"Shopping," James repeated slowly. This was probably his least favorite thing to do. He avoided the malls whenever possible. "But why?" he asked innocently. He wasn't giving in without a fight.

"Clothes," she informed him, then added in case he hadn't figured it out, "for you."

He frowned. Summer saw this and read his decided lack of enthusiasm for this project.

"You don't need to do this. I think you look wonderful in a suit and tie, but you'd be far more comfortable in jeans and a short-sleeve shirt."

So this was what she meant about altering his attitude. He noticed she hadn't mentioned working on his perspective meant torturing him by dragging him in and out of a dozen stores or more.

"James?" She looked up at him with eyes that would melt a felon's heart. "What's it to be?"

It was on the tip of his tongue to tell her he was perfectly relaxed with what he was wearing. He would have said it, too, if she hadn't blinked just then and her long, silky lashes fanned her cheek. Without much effort this woman was going to wrap his heart around her little finger. James could see it coming, but he hadn't the gumption to offer so much as a token resistance.

"How long will it take?" he asked, and glanced at his watch. He hoped to give the impression that the burros only made their appearance at certain times. They did. The minute they suspected someone had something edible with them, the donkeys appeared.

"We won't take more than an hour or two," she promised.

He was being fed a line and knew it. They'd be lucky to make Red Rock Canyon before nightfall.

"All right." What he needed, James decided, was a good counselor. Someone who could explain to him how a mature, reasonable male would allow a woman he barely knew dictate his wardrobe.

He hadn't a clue what was happening to him. Summer was several years too young for him, although it made her fighting mad every time he mentioned it. Age, however, was the least of his concerns.

She lived and worked in southern California. His life was in Seattle. He didn't know much about acting, but it seemed to him that if she was serious about her career, and she certainly seemed to be, then California was the place to be. Long-distance relationships rarely survived.

"You won't regret this," she said, and beamed him a smile.

She was wrong. James already regretted it.

When it came to shopping, James had no patience. The only shopping mall he knew about in Vegas was the one located on the strip between two of the largest casinos. He drove there and pulled into the underground-parking area.

When he turned off the ignition, Summer leaned over and kissed him.

"What was that for?" he asked, knowing full well he should be counting his blessings instead of questioning his good fortune.

"To thank you for being such a good sport."

Little did she know.

To his surprise, Summer was good to her word. It took all of two hours for her to locate everything she felt was necessary for him. James followed her around like a dutiful child, and to his amazement he discovered he enjoyed himself. Mostly he let her choose for him, and she did well, opting for styles he might have picked himself.

"I feel like I squeak when I walk," he said as he led the way back into the underground garage. Everything he had on was new. Right down to the shoes and socks.

"You look ten years younger," Summer told him.

"In which case you could be accused of cradle robbing."

Summer laughed and wrapped her arm around his and squeezed lightly. She pressed her head against his shoulder. James derived a good deal of pleasure in having her this close. He was still trying to figure out how he was going to manage to keep his hands off her. Having her wrap herself all over him wasn't helping matters any. The woman hadn't a clue about what she did to him.

"Sometimes it feels like I've known you forever," she whispered.

James had the same feeling. It was as if she'd been a part of his life for a very long time. "I have the feeling I'm going to have a large long-distance phone bill once I get back to Seattle."

Summer closed her eyes and sighed deeply.

"What was that all about?" He unlocked the car door and loaded the shopping bags into the back seat.

"I'm grateful is all," Summer told him.

"Grateful?" James asked, joining her inside the car.

She was quiet for a moment, as if needing time to gather her thoughts. "I don't respond this way with other men...the way I have with you. I can't offer you a reason or a logical explanation. In the last year since we've been writing, I've felt close to you. It's as if you know all there is to know about me. My secrets, my faults, everything.

"That night a year ago...when we first met, was probably the most devastating of my life. I don't know what I would have done if it hadn't been for you. Generally I'm the first person to dismiss this sort of thing, but I believe we were destined to meet."

James had wondered about that himself, although he'd never voiced his opinion. Out of all the people in that massive New Year's crowd, it boggled the mind that they should find each other. It had to mean something. He didn't doubt that fate, kismet or whatever it was had brought them together.

"I've never experienced the things I do when you kiss me."

She wasn't alone in that, either. He started the engine and pulled into the heavy traffic that continuously flowed along the strip. It helped to concentrate on his driving rather than look at Summer.

If they'd stayed in the parking garage much longer, James feared they'd have had a repeat performance from the night before.

Touching her breasts had been a big mistake because now the vision of her nipples tormented him. He'd spent half the night fighting off the image of her in bed with him, her legs wrapped around his waist. If he took any more cold showers, the hotel was going to complain about the amount of water he used.

Summer's voice was soft and unsure when she spoke. "I was convinced after last evening that you wouldn't want to see me again."

James nearly drove the car off the road. "That's ridiculous. Why would you think anything of the sort?"

She lowered her gaze to her hands, which were folded primly in her lap. "Well, for one thing, I behaved like a regular brazen."

"You?" The woman hadn't a clue how close he'd come to losing control in the front seat of a rental car. She didn't understand. Superior court judges didn't lose control. James couldn't remember the last time he'd allowed something like this to happen. If anyone should be accused of being impertinent, it was him.

"It does my heart good to know I'm not in this alone. I don't think I could bear that."

"Trust me, I'm experiencing many of the same feelings you are," he told her in what had to be the understatement of the century.

"I didn't know what to think. We'll both be going our separate ways within the next few days. Frankly, until just now, I didn't know if I'd ever hear from you again. That was what my sigh was about."

"We've been in touch all year—why would that end now?" He didn't expect anything permanent to develop between them; that would be asking too much.

"We can take turns phoning each other," she offered.

"All right," he agreed, but he was old-fashioned enough to want to do the calling himself.

Summer was silent following that, and he was beginning to recognize quiet moments as a sign of trouble. "What's wrong?"

She glanced at him and smiled softly. "I was just thinking that it would be nice to see each other every once in a while, as well. I hope I don't sound pushy."

Seeing her on a regular basis suited him just fine. They hadn't even gone their separate ways, and already James anticipated withdrawal problems. It would be damn easy to grow accustomed to having Summer with him.

"I could fly up and visit you one month, and you could fly down and visit me the next," she suggested, again sounding uncertain.

James's hands tightened around the steering wheel. He strongly suspected it would be easier to wean himself off drugs than to torture himself by leaving Summer on a monthly basis.

"You're not saying anything."

"I was mulling matters over. I do that quite a bit, Summer."

"What were you thinking?"

The complete truth would have embarrassed them both. "I was mentally reviewing my schedule." The primary wasn't scheduled until September, but Ralph Southworth, a longtime businessman and friend who'd agreed to head up James's campaign, had made it clear to him long ago. From here on out, James's life wasn't his own. Every place James went, every civic event he attended, would be a campaigning opportunity.

"And?" Summer prompted.

"February might be difficult for me to get away." His work load had suffered with this vacation, and another trip, however brief, so soon afterward could cause additional problems.

"That's all right, I can come to you. In fact, I've probably got enough frequent-flyer miles to make the trip free."

"Great. Then I'll make an effort to see you in March."

"Wonderful." She lit up like a sparkler on the Fourth of July, then hesitated and bit into her lower lip. "April might be a problem. Disneyland stays open until midnight during spring break, and we add a second *Beauty and the Beast* show in the evenings. It's difficult to get a free weekend."

"We can work around that." He didn't want to mention that from June onward his schedule would be impossible. There was no possibility of his visiting California, and if she was able to come to Seattle, he couldn't guarantee he could make the time to spend with her.

"We can work around any obstacle," she said, but she didn't sound overly optimistic.

They were outside the city now, heading along a two-lane highway that led toward Red Rock Canyon. "I'll be heavily involved in my campaign this summer." He didn't feel he could be any less than honest.

"Summer is the busiest time of year for me, as well," she said with an air of defeat. "But we can make this work, James, if we both want it bad enough."

It frightened him how badly he wanted Summer, but he was enough of a realist to point out the obvious. "Long-distance relationships rarely work."

"Is that a fact? I take it you've been involved in several and speak from experience?"

James resisted the urge to laugh at her prim tone of voice. If memory served him right, his first-grade teacher, Mrs. Bondi, used precisely that tone. Come to think of it, he'd been in love with her, too.

"You'd be shocked by how few relationships I've been in," he confessed.

"Do we have a relationship?" Summer asked softly.

James certainly hoped so. "Yes," he answered, and then because she seemed to need convincing, he pulled onto a dirt road and behind a ten-foot-high rock. A trail of red dust plumed behind them.

"Why are you stopping?" she asked.

James wore a wide grin and held out his arms to her. "It appears to me you need a little reminder of how involved we are." James knew he was asking for trouble. Trouble with a capital *T.* His resistance was probably about as weak as it could get. He hadn't the strength to fight her any longer.

"Oh, James."

"A few kisses is all, understand? I don't have much willpower when it comes to you."

"You don't?" The words were whispered. "That's probably the most beautiful thing you've ever said to me."

"Has anyone ever told you, you talk too much," James said as his mouth swooped down on hers. He kissed her the way he'd been wanting to all morning, hell, from the moment he'd watched her approach him in the gazebo.

It felt as if it had been a thousand years since he'd held her in his arms, far longer than it should have been, far longer than he ever cared to wait again.

He kissed her again and again, unable to get his fill. He demanded and she gave. He moaned and she sighed. It was then and there James decided that he'd do whatever possible, move heaven and earth, fly a red-eye special to be with her. He sincerely doubted once a month would be near enough.

His tongue met hers, and the two became involved in a slow, carnal pursuit that left James panting. He ached to touch her breasts, until it became a physical pain.

In an effort to occupy his hands, he plowed them into her hair and sifted the long strands through his fingers. With their mouths still joined, he lowered one hand to the slim column of her throat and found her pulse. It beat savagely against the tip of his fingers.

The urge to fill his palms with her breasts was overwhelming. James had never thought of himself as a weak man. But with Summer he felt as hot and uncontrollable as a seventeen-year-old in the front seat of his daddy's car.

Nothing was enough for him. He could have buried himself hip deep into her softness, and it wouldn't have satisfied him. Frankly James didn't know what would.

Her breasts were flattened against his chest, which was probably safest, James decided, in light of how he was feeling. Reluctantly he dragged his mouth from hers and trailed moist kisses along the side of her neck. He located her pulse point with his tongue and pressed it there, loving the strong, flagrant beat of her heart.

"James."

"Hmm?" He rushed his mouth back to hers, kissing her slow and easy. Talking was the last thing on his mind.

"James." She tried again, his name much weaker this time.

Unable to resist any longer, he fumbled with the small buttons of her blouse, his fingers shaking in his eagerness to free her breasts. The fantasy that had kept him awake half the night was about to become reality.

"We seem . . ." she whispered breathlessly.

James's hands were behind her back, reaching for the snap of her bra that would release her bounty.

". . . to have company."

James went still. When he'd left the roadway, he'd made sure they were out of sight. Sweet heaven, he couldn't believe he was doing this. "Company?" he repeated. Already he could see the headlines. King County Superior Court judge caught in compromising position in car with show girl while in Vegas.

"They look hungry, too."

James's gaze followed Summer's. Burros, four or five of them, stood outside the car, intently studying them. They were patiently waiting for a handout.

James relaxed and grinned. At least the wild burros didn't carry a camera.

Summer smiled, as well.

"I brought along a loaf of bread," he said, and reached into the seat behind him.

Summer leaned forward enough to secure her bra and refasten her blouse. "Should we get out of the car?" she asked.

"I don't think that's a good idea." He'd read about the friendly burros, but he wasn't sure how tame they were. "Perhaps it would be best to roll down the window a bit and feed them that way."

"Good idea." Summer opened her window a couple of inches, enough to ease a slice of bread out to eager mouths. Exactly how eager was something they were to quickly learn.

"Oh, my," Summer cried, backing away from the window.

James glanced her way to find a large tongue making its way into the small opening.

Soon they were both laughing and dishing up the bread as fast as their hands would work. James didn't know what they'd do when the bread ran out, but Summer certainly seemed to be enjoying herself. It was difficult for him to keep his mind on the task. The temptation was far stronger to watch Summer.

When the loaf ran out, Summer and James rolled up the windows. It took several moments for the burros to realize their food supply had run dry.

When the burros left, James started the engine and pulled back onto the road. They drove for another hour, stopped and toured a visitors' center and took in the beauty of the countryside.

James felt Summer staring at him as he drove back toward the city.

"Now what?" he asked.

"I can't get over the change in you."

"You mean the clothes?"

"Yes. You look like a Jim instead of a James."

James grinned. "There's a difference?"

"Oh, yes, a very big one."

"Which do you prefer?" he asked, studying her from the corner of his eye. Actually he found this all to be rather amusing.

His question appeared to give her some hesitation. "I'm not sure. I like the way Jim dresses, but I like the way James kisses."

"What about how Jim kisses?" The conversation was touching upon the ridiculous.

"Too impatient, I think."

"Really?" He couldn't help being slightly miffed. "What's so wonderful about James?"

"The restraint. When James kisses me, it's as if he were holding back a part of himself. I have the feeling he's afraid to let go, and it drives me crazy wanting to discover what he's hiding from me. I know all this probably sounds a little nutso, but I find James intriguing."

So much for those who claim the clothes don't make the man.

"And Jim?"

She giggled. "Don't tell him, but he's sexy as hell."

"Really?" James was beginning to feel downright cocky.

"He's got that devil-may-care attitude. I have a strong feeling we should be grateful to those burros, because there's no telling what could have developed between us in the canyon."

She was right about that.

"It's those tennis shoes you insisted I buy," James told her. "The minute I slipped my foot inside that shoe, a new persona came over me. I had this incredible urge to find a basketball court and do slam dunks." James loved the sound of Summer's laugher. He'd never been one to tease and joke, but he'd soon learn if he was rewarded with her appreciation for his wit.

It was mid-afternoon by the time they arrived back at the hotel. After showing the security guard their keys, they stepped into the elevator.

"How about dinner together later?" he asked, hoping he sounded cool and casual when in reality his heart dangled from his sleeve.

"Sure, what time?"

"Six," he suggested. Three hours, and he'd be more than ready to see her again. He'd like to suggest they do something until then, but didn't want to monopolize her time, although he'd pretty much succeeded in doing that anyway.

"Six o'clock. In the lobby?"

"The lobby," he agreed.

The elevator arrived at her floor, and Summer stared down at her room key. "I'll see you at six."

"Six." They sounded like a pair of parrots.

"Thanks for taking me along this morning," she said, easing toward the door.

"Thank you." He bounced an imaginary basketball and pretended to make a hoop shot.

She smiled, and acting on pure instinct, James lowered his mouth to hers and kissed her. It was gentle and tender and sweet and when they broke apart, it was all James could do not to follow her to her room.

Summer sat on the end of her bed, her hands trembling. She closed her eyes and attempted to relive those last seconds with James and couldn't. Being in his arms was the only possible way to recapture the incredible sensation she experienced each time she was with him.

Julie, her roommate, had known long before Summer had realized it herself. When James had asked her how often she dated, she'd invented a variety of excuses why her social life was nonexistent of late.

But it was really because of his letters.

Hearing from James had become the most important part of her life. Each month she rushed to the mailbox, knowing there'd be a long letter from him.

She'd fallen in love with the gentle, tender man who'd written her those beautiful letters.

Unfortunately she hadn't realized it until she'd seen James. At first she worried that she alone experienced all this feeling, all this awareness. After the way he'd kissed her, she knew that couldn't be true. He felt it, too. Like being hit by a Mack truck, James felt it.

She smiled to herself, remembering how flustered he'd looked when she'd announced they had an audience.

Summer had been disconcerted herself, but nothing like James, who looked as if he was about to rip apart with his bare hands any man or woman who dared intrude upon them.

Summer's face broke into a smile at the memory.

Lying down on the bed, she stared up at the ceiling and soon found herself giggling. She was in love with James. Even now it took some getting used to. To think she'd so strongly believed she'd never love another man after Jason.

She might have drowned in a pool of self-pity if it hadn't been for James. She owed him so much.

In thinking over their plans to continue seeing each other, she knew it would be difficult for them to maintain the relationship, especially when they lived separate lives.

It would take effort and commitment on both their parts. Summer was willing. James wasn't as convinced as she was that they could make a go of this, but she didn't harbor a single doubt.

Summer dressed carefully for her dinner date with James. She chose a dirndl with a pretty white blouse that laced up the front. She left the front ties loose, exposing a bit of cleavage. Past experience had taught her that James appreciated her breasts.

He was waiting at the same place in the lobby, but he surprised her by not wearing a suit and tie. He opted for one of the short-sleeve shirts with a V-necked sweater. For a moment she barely recognized him. He looked relaxed, as though he hadn't a care in the world.

"James," she whispered when she joined him.

"Jim," he corrected, and grinned. He placed his hand inside his pant pocket and struck a catalog pose.

Summer laughed outright.

"I hope you're hungry," James said. He tucked her hand in the crook of his elbow and guided her toward the door.

"I'm starved." Summer hadn't eaten lunch, and her stomach wouldn't soon forgive her.

"Great. We're about to indulge ourselves in a feast fit for the gods." When they reached the sidewalk of Glitter Gulch, the lights made it as light as the noonday sun.

"I thought about our conversation from this afternoon," he announced out of the blue.

"About keeping in touch?" she asked.

He nodded and she noted how serious his dark eyes had become. Apparently the subject had been heavy on his mind. "I'm not sure what we have, but whatever it is, I don't want to lose it."

"I don't, either."

"I've only felt this strongly about one other woman in my life."

"I've only felt this way about one other person," she admitted.

"If I were looking to put a name on what's between us . . ."

"Yes," she prodded when he hesitated. James was a deep, thoughtful man. She didn't mean to rush him, but she wanted him to say what was already on the tip of her tongue. When he paused, she had no qualms about leaping in with both feet. "I love you, James Wilkens. My heart is so full I can barely walk. I want to throw my arms in the air and sing."

He looked at her as if he were actually afraid she would do exactly that. "What you feel is gratitude."

"Gratitude," she repeated as if it were a four-letter word. "I'm capable of knowing my own mind, thank you kindly, and when I say I love you, I mean it."

"I see," James said, and his voice dipped considerably.

"You don't need to worry about telling me how you feel, either," she was quick to assure him. It wasn't necessary; his kiss told her everything she needed to know.

"If you must know."

"It isn't necessary." She stopped in the middle of the crowded sidewalk and pressed her finger to his lips.

"I'm too damn old for you."

Her gaze narrowed.

"But I'm crazy about you, Summer. Call me the biggest damn fool that ever lived, but it's true."

"Thank you very much."

James chuckled. "I haven't been doing a very good job of hiding how I feel. I didn't expect this." He splayed his fingers through his hair. "In retrospect, I wonder what I did expect."

"I assumed we'd have dinner that first night and I'd tell you everything I already hadn't in my letters, and then we'd more or less go our separate ways."

"Really." He arched his eyebrows.

"I wanted Julie to fly in for the weekend, but she refused and I never could get her to give me a reason why. I know now. My feelings for you aren't new. They slowly developed over the last year. I don't want to lose you, James. We can make this work if we try."

"It's not going to be easy."

His words started to fade as an idea struck Summer. "Oh, my goodness." She pressed the tips of her fingers to her mouth.

James stopped abruptly. "What is it?"

"James." Her hand gripped hold of his arm as she stared up at him. With every passing second the idea gained momentum. "I just thought of something...wonderful."

"Do you need to sit down?" His arm circled her waist.

"No...no, I'm fine. Oh, James. Kiss me, please, just kiss me." She felt as though she were about to burst.

"Kiss you here?" James asked, appalled.

"Never mind." She laughed, and, looping her arms around his neck, she stood on the tips of her toes and kissed him. It was a deep, lingering kiss that told her everything she needed to know.

He stared down at her dumbstruck when she'd finished.

"James," she said breathlessly, "I think we should get married."

"Married," he repeated. The word was barely audible.

"It makes perfect sense, don't you think? I know how I feel about you, and you just admitted your feelings for me. Here we are both worried about the most ridiculous things, when we already have what's most important. Each other."

Still James didn't say anything. He looked around as if he needed a good, stiff drink. He went pale, but that could have been her imagination.

"I already know what you're thinking," she said with a laugh, "but I've got an answer for every one of your arguments."

"We barely know each other."

That was a pretty weak argument. "Is that so? You know me better than friends I've had all my life. You've seen me at my very worst. You've listened to my pain and answered my frustrations. I don't feel like there's a thing I can't talk over with you."

He frowned the most intense frown Summer had ever seen. She longed to soothe the lines from his troubled brow and kiss away his doubts.

"Don't look so worried. Honestly, James, one would think you were in a state of shock."

"I am." This came through loud and clear.

"But why?" His hesitation took her by surprise. She knew the idea would take some getting used to on James's part. He didn't leap into projects and ideas the way she did. He was methodical and thoughtful and carefully weighed every decision.

"Perhaps I'm assuming something here that I shouldn't," she said slowly, thoughtfully. All at once Summer felt as though she were about to be sick. It made perfect sense.

"You don't want to marry me, do you, James?"

Chapter Four

Summer was mortified to the very marrow of her bones. Without even trying, she'd managed to make a complete fool of herself. James had never come right out and said he was in love with her. With all their talk about how important they were to each other, she'd naturally assumed he cared as deeply for her as she did him. She'd assumed he'd want to marry her.

"James, I'm sorry," she said in a voice no stronger than a reed. Past experience had taught her to right the wrong as quickly as possible.

"Summer..."

"Of course you don't want to marry me. I understand, really, I do," she said, and pretended to laugh, but it came out sounding more like a muffled sob. "Now I've embarrassed us both. I don't know why I say the ridiculous things I do." She tried to make light of it by gesturing with her hands. "I guess I should have warned you that I blurt out the most incredibly awkward things. Forget I said anything about marriage, please—otherwise it'll ruin our evening.''

James was silent, which made everything ten times worse. She'd rather he ranted and raved than said nothing.

In an effort to fill the terrible silence, she started chattering, talking ten miles per hour and saying virtually nothing, bouncing without rhyme or reason from one subject to another.

She commented on how busy the casinos were this time of the evening. She talked about the big-name stars performing in town. She mentioned the name of a friend of a friend who'd won the California State lottery, and the air-pollution problems in the Los Angeles area.

"Summer, stop," James told her softly. "It's fine."

She snapped her mouth closed so fast her teeth clicked as they hit against each other. How she was going to make it through the evening without humiliating herself further, she didn't know.

Her stomach was in such a knot that by the time they reached the restaurant, she was convinced she'd only be able to make a pretense of eating.

The hostess seated them, but Summer couldn't have named the restaurant had her life depended on it.

"If you'll excuse me," she said as soon as the hostess left them.

James looked up from the menu.

"I'll be right back." She was hoping that a few minutes alone in the ladies' room would help her gather her composure.

"Summer," James said in that reserved way of his, "I don't want you to feel badly about this."

She nodded, preferring to drop the subject entirely. "Did you notice they had lobster on the menu?" She hadn't a clue if this was true or not.

"It's just that a man prefers to do the asking."

"Of course." She agreed entirely, and it went without saying that the very proper King County Superior Court Judge James Wilkens wouldn't want an empty-headed actress for his wife.

Summer set the linen napkin aside and asked a passing waiter directions for the powder room. As she walked across the restaurant, weaving her way around tables, she felt James's eyes following her.

Once inside the ladies' room, Summer sat on the pink velvet sofa and closed her eyes. After drawing in a number of deep, calming breaths, she waited for the acute embarrassment to pass.

It didn't.

Briefly she toyed with the idea of silently slipping away, but that would have been childish and unfair to James. His only crime had been his silence, and he'd already explained that was simply his way. Just like making a world-class fool of herself seemed to be her trademark.

Five minutes later she rejoined him.

He looked up almost as if he were surprised to see her. "I wasn't sure you'd be back."

"I wouldn't be that rude. It isn't your fault I'm an idiot."

"Stop," he said sharply. "I won't have you saying such things about yourself."

"Like you're going to marry someone like me?" she said, poking fun at herself. "What a joke."

"As a matter of fact, I do plan on marrying you." He announced this while scanning the menu, which he promptly set aside. He looked over at her as if he expected some kind of argument. Summer might have offered him one if her throat hadn't closed up on her like a vise, making talking and breathing impossible.

The menu slipped from her fingers and fell onto the table. Nervously she groped for it.

"Have you decided?" James asked.

She stared at him blankly.

"What would you like to order for dinner?"

"Oh." She hadn't so much as looked. Frazzled as she was, she opted for the first thing she saw. "Chicken dijon," she said.

"Not lobster? It isn't every day one becomes engaged. I think we should celebrate, don't you?"

Somehow she managed the weakest of nods.

The waiter came, and James ordered for them both, requesting lobster and champagne. Their server nodded approvingly and disappeared. Momentarily he returned with a champagne bottle for James's inspection.

"We'll need to see about an engagement ring," James said as though they were discussing something as mundane as the weather. "I imagine Las Vegas has a number of good jewelers."

The waiter opened the champagne bottle with a loud pop and poured a small amount into the fluted glass for James to sample. He tasted it and nodded. Soon both their glasses were filled.

Summer breathed easier once they were alone. "James," she whispered, leaning against the edge of the table, "are you sure you want to marry me?"

He leaned toward her, pressing his torso against the side of the table. A slow, easy grin formed over his mouth. "Yes."

"All at once I'm not so sure I'm the right person for you."

"Shouldn't I be the one to decide that?"

"Yes, but…I'd hate to think that we're reacting to a bunch of circumstances that wouldn't repeat themselves in a hundred years."

"Then we'll have a long engagement. We'll both be very sure before we take that one final step."

"All right." Summer felt only mildly reassured.

"We'll continue to see each other on a regular basis," James assured her.

"Yes…we'll need that." She didn't like the idea of their being apart so much of the time, but that couldn't be helped.

"I wouldn't want the engagement to be too long," Summer said. "I dated Jason for five years, and we were unofficially and officially engaged almost that entire time. We both know what happened."

"Do you wish you'd married him?"

"No," she answered emphatically. "I don't have a single regret when it comes to Jason. I was young and foolish…you'd never do the things Jason did."

James's eyes brightened with intensity. "It isn't in me to hurt you."

"Or me you," she added in a gentle whisper.

"In light of what happened between Christy and me, I'm not necessarily fond of long engagements, either."

"In reviewing your engagement with Christy, do you regret not marrying her sooner? That way she would have gone to visit her sister as a married woman."

"I've thought about that a number of times," James said without hesitating. "Christy would never have allowed anything to develop between her and Cody had we already been married. Dating him behind my back was almost more than she could bear.''

"I see." Summer could read the handwriting on the wall. "You wish you'd married her, don't you?"

"No."

His quick response surprised her. "Why not?"

"Christy Manning didn't love me with the same intensity that I loved her. I'm sure she would have done her best to be a good wife, and we probably would have grown close over the years, but she'd have married me for the wrong reasons."

"The wrong reasons?"

"She was looking to make her parents happy."

"Okay," Summer said slowly, still feeling her way carefully around the subject. "So neither of us wants a long engagement. How long is long? A year?"

"Too long," James said with feeling.

"Six months?"

He hesitated. "That'll be June."

"June's a nice month," Summer said without any real enthusiasm. "Will you want me to live with you in Seattle?"

"Of course. Is that a problem?"

"None," she was quick to assure him.

"What about your career?"

She lifted one shoulder. "To tell you the truth, I was a little sick of playing Belle anyway. From what I understand, Seattle's live theater is thriving. There wouldn't be any problem with me being your wife and an actress, would there? You being a judge and all."

"None that I can think of."

"Good." Summer picked up her fork and ran her fingers along the smooth tines. "My current contract with Disney expires in April."

"April," James said. "Can you arrange a wedding on such short notice?"

"You'd be surprised what I could arrange," she said. Her heart felt worlds lighter. "Oh, James, I can't believe this is happening."

"To be honest, neither can I," he admitted.

Summer didn't know when she'd seen him smile brighter.

The waiter delivered their dinner, and James looked at the man who was a complete stranger and said, "The young lady and I have decided to marry."

Their server smiled broadly. "Congratulations."

"Thank you."

Summer would have added her thanks, but James had shocked her speechless. He wasn't joking; he really meant to follow through with their wedding and he was excited about it. Excited enough to announce their plans to a stranger.

"The hotel has an excellent wedding chapel," the waiter continued. "From what I understand, more than one celebrity has been married in our chapel."

"Right here in the hotel?" James asked.

"Many of the larger hotels provide wedding services for their guests."

"The arrangements must be made weeks in advance."

"Not always," the waiter explained. "A lot of people don't decide which chapel to use until after they arrive. From what I understand, a person can marry with as little as a few hours' notice, if the wedding chapel's available, of course."

"Naturally," James commented.

A funny look came over him, and Summer didn't know what to think. "Our wedding will be in April," she supplied.

"My very best to the both of you," the waiter said, and refilled their flutes with champagne.

"James," Summer said after the server had left their table, "is something wrong?"

"Nothing. What makes you ask?"

"You're wearing that look."

"What look?"

"The one that says you're not sure you like what you're thinking or hearing or seeing. It was the one you got when I mentioned we had company the other day in Red Rock Canyon."

"I can't believe what I'm thinking."

"You want to call off the wedding?" She should have realized that when James said he wanted to marry her it was too good to be true. This had to be the shortest engagement in history.

"I don't know where you get the idea I'm looking for a way out of this when I'm thinking exactly the opposite. I can only assume impulsive thoughts must be transmitted from one brain to another."

"Impulsive thoughts?"

"Yes." He drew in a deep breath and seemed to hold it for a long time. "Would you be willing to marry me now?"

"Now?"

"Then repeat the ceremony later with family and friends in April."

To be shocked speechless happened rarely with Summer, and yet James had managed to do it twice in the same evening. She stared at him, and her mouth opened and closed two or three times, but no words came out.

"Summer, have I utterly shocked you?"

"Yes," she admitted in a squeaky, high voice.

James grinned broadly. "I'll admit this is the first impulsive thought I've entertained in years. If you can propose marriage at the drop of a hat, then I should be able to come up with something equally thrilling."

Summer knew she was going to cry now. Already she could feel the tears crowd the edges of her eyes. She used her linen napkin to dab away the liquid.

"Just remember when we tell the children about this night. You're the one who proposed to me."

"Children." Summer blew her nose. "Oh, James, I'm so anxious to be a mother."

"Then you agree to my plan?"

"Marry twice?" Everything was going too fast for her. "I'd want Julie here as my maid of honor."

"Of course. We can phone her as soon as we're finished with dinner. If it's a problem, I'll pay for her airfare."

The tears were back, filling the edges of her eyes, but these were happy tears because she loved him so much. "James, we're doing the right thing, aren't we?"

He didn't hesitate. "Yes. It's what we both want."

"You love me?" He'd never said the words, not once.

His look softened. "Very much."

Her mind buzzed with all the things they'd need to do. "I'll have to tell my parents. You didn't intend to keep our marriage a secret from family, did you?"

"No. I'll contact my father, as well."

Already Summer could hear her mother argue with her. "They're going to think we're crazy."

James grinned. "Probably."

Summer didn't remember the rest of what they said over dinner.

"What should we do first?" Summer asked as they left the restaurant.

"I suppose we should find the first available wedding chapel."

"Shouldn't we contact our families before we do that?" This was the part Summer dreaded most, and she wanted it over as quickly as possible. "But then, if we have the chapel booked, we'll be able to tell them the time and place."

"Exactly. The ring," James said, and snapped his fingers. "I almost forgot that."

"Don't look so concerned. We can pick something out later. A plain gold band is perfect for now. In April we can exchange those for a diamond if you want."

"I'd like you to have my mother's ring."

"I'd be honored and proud to wear it."

He kissed her gently, and Summer blinked back her surprise. It was the first time he'd ever kissed her in public.

Since the waiter had mentioned the wedding chapel at the hotel, they tried there first. Summer wasn't sure what she expected, but booking their wedding took only a matter of minutes. The hotel saw to everything, from obtaining the license to the music and flowers.

"That was easy," James commented as they walked back to the Four Queens. "If I'd known it was this simple, I might have suggested it sooner."

Summer pressed her head against his shoulder. They stopped at a crosswalk and waited for the red light.

"I wish you'd kiss me again," she breathed close to his ear.

His gaze found her lips, and he cleared his throat. "I don't think that would be a good idea."

"I suppose you're right." She agreed with him. Public displays of affection were frowned upon, but disappointment underscored her words.

"You can call your family from my room."

"Okay," she said, but her mind wasn't on making the dreaded phone call as much as it was on being alone with James.

His thoughts must have been along the same lines because their pace quickened as they hurried across the street and into the hotel.

The elevator ride seemed to take an eternity. As if James couldn't keep himself from touching her in some way, he reached out and brushed a stray curl away from her cheek. His knuckle grazed her smooth skin.

"I can't believe you're willing to marry me," he said.

"I feel like the luckiest woman alive."

"You?" He held his hand to his brow. "I want you so damn much I think I'm running a fever."

"I've got a fever, too, James. Oh, James, we're going to be so good for one another. I promise to be a good wife to you."

"Don't," he growled.

"Don't?" She couldn't help having her feelings hurt.

"Don't look at me like that, Summer. I'm weak enough where you're concerned. Much more of this, and I'm going to make love to you right in this elevator."

Summer smiled and leaned against the back of the elevator car. "You're incredibly romantic, James Wilkens."

"You're doing it again."

"Doing what?"

"Looking at me like you know exactly what I want. Your eyes are telling me you want it as much as I do."

She untied the front of her blouse and loosened the strings, exposing the deep valley between her lush breasts. "I do know what you want."

The elevator car eased to a stop, and the doors slid open. Summer's heart pounded fast and hard, and neither made the slightest effort to leave.

"We were going to call our families," she reminded him.

The Adam's apple in James's throat moved up and down. "Yes, of course."

With crisp, precise movements he led the way out of the elevator and down the hallway to his room. She noticed when he inserted the key into the lock that his hand trembled slightly, and she loved him all the more for it.

"The phone's over by the..."

"Bed," she completed the thought for him, and the word stuck in her throat. She walked across the room and sat on the edge of the mattress and dialed the familiar number to her parents' home.

It would have helped had she taken the time to give some thought to the matter of what she intended to say. But she was afraid she'd lose her nerve.

It wasn't possible to put into words what she felt for James. She'd never loved this way before, and she believed he hadn't, either. Each had been in love with someone else, and that other person had been responsible for deep pain. This time was different. This time was ordained by a power greater than themselves. Summer was convinced of that.

Her love for James was so intense that when she thought about him, a feeling so strong and powerful welled up inside her that she could barely breathe.

She knew, even before they picked up the phone, what her mother and father were going to say. The arguments lined up like soldiers prepared for a long march.

"James," she said, her voice in a panic. She replaced the telephone receiver and held out her arms to him. "Please, could you kiss me first?"

She looked over to the man she would marry in less than twenty-four hours, and his face was a study of raw sexual need. He walked across the room. The mattress dipped as his weight joined hers. With loving care he gathered her in his arms and claimed her mouth. The kiss was slow and sensual. Soon his tongue was seeking out hers, sipping and savoring, seducing her.

He broke away, and his breath came hard and labored. Her own was broken and uneven. Eager for the taste of him, the touch and feel of him, she brushed her lips over the curve of his jaw.

James directed her mouth back to his. This kiss was long and moist. He moved her back onto the mattress and spread out next to her.

Summer rubbed the lower half of her body provocatively against him and smiled at his thick, ready response.

"Summer," he breathed as if in agony. His hands gripped hold of her hips to still her. "Stop," he pleaded. "I knew I'd never last another four months without making love to you, but I did think I could last twenty-four hours."

"Maybe you should contact your father first."

"All right," he agreed. Reluctantly he sat up and reached for the phone. Summer knelt behind him, wrapped her arms around his torso and pressed her head against his shoulder.

"Dad, it's James," she heard him say.

"Fine...yes, Vegas is just fine." Summer could hear a voice on the other end of the line, but she couldn't make out what was being said.

"I'm calling to let you know I'm getting married."

The voice went silent.

"Dad? Are you still there?"

The faraway voice returned, this time speaking very fast.

"Dad...Dad...Dad." Three times James tried to cut in and each time was prevented from saying anything more than his father's name.

In frustration, James held the phone away from his ear. "I think you'd better talk to him."

"Me?" Summer cried. "What do you want me to say?"

"Anything."

Summer took the receiver and pressed her hand over the mouthpiece. "Just remember this when we talk to my parents."

"I will." He kissed her briefly.

"Mr. Wilkens," Summer said softly. The line sounded as if it had suddenly gone dead. "My name's

Summer Lawton. James and I have known each other a year. I love him very, very much.''

"If you've known my son for one year, how is it we've never met?"

"I live in California."

"California?"

"Orange County. I'm an actress." She might as well give him all the bad news at one time. Summer didn't dare look at James, certain he'd rather not blurt out everything.

"An actress?"

"That's correct."

"You're sure you've got the right James Wilkens? My son's the superior court judge."

"Yes, I know. James and I are going to be married tomorrow evening at seven but we're planning a much larger ceremony later in April. As his father, we felt it was only right we tell you about our plans." Convinced she'd done a miserable job, Summer handed the telephone back to James.

Father and son talked a few moments more, and the conversation ended with James abruptly replacing the telephone receiver. He looked at Summer, but she had the strangest feeling he wasn't seeing her.

"James?"

"He's decided to fly in for the ceremony."

"That's great. I'll look forward to meeting him."

"He's anxious to meet you, as well. He hasn't set eyes on you and already he thinks you're the best thing that's ever happened to me."

Summer laughed and looped her arms around James's neck. "He could be right."

James grinned up at her. "I know he is." Slowly his gaze traveled from her mouth to her breasts. The ties

Summer had loosened earlier were slack now, revealing velvet-smooth skin. "You aren't wearing a bra," he said, and his gaze seared her.

"Yes, I know. Generally everything is tucked neatly into place, and one isn't necessary." She reached behind her back for the zipper. The teeth made a slow hissing sound as the zipper opened.

"Summer."

She peeled the jumper from her arms. The blouse was all that stood between her and the smooth, silky skin of her opulent breasts.

"Summer?"

She breathed deeply, and her rounded chest rose and fell with the action. James groaned, and the sound was one of deep, male need. As though he couldn't wait one moment longer to touch her, he sought the swell of her breasts, filling his palms with her bounty.

Her nipples beaded instantly and jutted out with pride against the thin cotton fabric. He made a rough sound again, one that was almost like a growl, and lifted the blouse from her, pulling it over her head.

Summer was afraid she might feel self-conscious, bare breasted. James's raptured gaze didn't leave her.

"You're beautiful."

Summer closed her eyes as his mouth, wet and warm, slid across her breast and fastened onto a tight nipple. She sucked in a deep breath at the fury of wild, hot sensation that shot through her. He plundered her breast, and she arched toward him, offering him everything she had to give.

"You'd test the very saints," James whispered, his shoulders heaving as he struggled to marshal his control. "Soon, my love, very, very soon."

Summer was witness to the strength of will he possessed. The effort it cost him to move away from her appeared to drain him of energy. He handed her back her blouse, helped her ease it over her head and personally saw to the tightening of the ties.

"We're going to tuck everything back where it belongs," he said sternly. "I haven't the strength to resist you, Summer. I'd appreciate your help."

"Out of sight, out of mind?" she said. From what she knew of James, she strongly suspected very little tested him to his limits. Knowing she did thrilled her.

He closed his eyes and nodded. "Something like that."

"I love you, James."

"I know. All I can say is that it's a damn good thing we're marrying now instead of later. I don't believe I could take much more of this."

Summer slipped back into the jumper top, and James zipped up the back. He handed her the telephone receiver when he was finished.

Summer had been delaying the inevitable and knew it. She stared at the phone, expelled a heavy sigh and said, "All right, I'll call my parents. Just be prepared, James, they're going to have a lot of questions."

"They couldn't be any worse than my father," he muttered.

"Wanna bet?" Summer punched out the number to the family home and waited. It was the decent thing to do, to contact her family with the news of her marriage, but if they just happened to be away... out of town themselves, no one would blame her and James for going through with the ceremony.

Four rings. Summer was just about to hang up.

"Hello," greeted her mother's cheerful voice.

"Mom," Summer said excitedly. "It's Summer."

"I thought you were in Vegas this week with Julie."

"Julie couldn't come."

"You went alone?" Already Summer could hear the disapproval in her mother's voice.

"I met a friend here. That's the reason I'm calling."

"Your friend? What's the matter? You don't sound right. You're gambling and you've lost everything and you want your father and me to mortgage the house?"

"Mom, it's nothing like that."

"I never did understand why you'd go back to Vegas after what happened to you there last year."

"Mom, can I explain?"

"All right, all right."

"I'm calling to tell you...."

"Don't beat around the bush, just say it."

Summer rolled her eyes. She knew where her flair for drama had come from. "I'm getting married."

Her mother screamed, and the next thing Summer heard was the phone dropping. Her father's voice could be heard in the background, followed by moaning and crying.

"What the hell's going on?" It was her father who came back on the line.

"Hi, Dad," Summer greeted as if nothing were awry. "I called to tell you and Mom that I'm getting married tomorrow evening."

Summer's father said nothing for several seconds. "Do we know this young man?"

"No. But he's wonderful, Dad, really wonderful."

"Like Jason was wonderful?" her mother shouted from the extension.

"Helen, get off the phone. You're too emotional to talk sense."

"Don't tell me what to do, Hank Lawton, this is our little girl who's marrying some stranger."

"His name's James Wilkens. He's from Seattle and, Daddy, I'm crazy about him, really crazy."

"He's an actor, isn't he?" her mother demanded. "What did I tell you over and over again? Stay away from actors. But do you listen to me?"

"Mom, James is a judge."

Silence.

"Mom, Dad, did you hear me?"

"What kind of judge? Beauty pageants?" This came from her mother.

"No. Superior court. He was recently appointed to the bench and will run for election to his first full term this November."

"A judge, Hank," Helen said softly. "Abby's daughter married that attorney, and we never heard the end of it. Summer's got herself a judge."

"Would you like to talk to James?" Summer offered. It only seemed fair he talk to her family, since he'd put her on the phone with his father.

"No," her father surprised her by saying. "When I talk to him, it'll be eye to eye. Pack our bags, Helen. We're headed for Vegas."

Chapter Five

"Sweetheart," James said patiently when he noted her distress, "what did you expect your family to do?"

"I didn't think they'd insist on being here," Summer answered. "I wanted it to be just you and me. We can involve our families later, in April. I felt obliged to let my parents know what we were doing...but I didn't expect anything like this."

"You don't want them to come?"

"No," she said quickly.

In some ways James could understand her regrets. If the truth be known, he'd have preferred it if his father stayed in Seattle. As it was, James's time with Summer was already limited, and he didn't want to share with family what precious few days they had left together.

"I'm afraid once you meet my mother, you'll change your mind about marrying me," she blurted out.

"Honey, it isn't possible."

"My mother...she sometimes doesn't think before she speaks."

"I see." James felt he was being diplomatic by not mentioning Summer possessed the identical trait.

"My dad's really great...you'll like him, but probably not at first." She looked to James with large, imploring eyes. "Oh, James, he's going to give you the fifth degree. I wouldn't doubt that he's having a background check done on you this very minute."

"I don't have anything to hide."

"You see, Dad's been working with the seamy side of life for so many years, he suspects everyone."

"He's a policeman?"

Summer nodded. "I don't think he trusts anyone."

"Sweetheart, if twenty-odd years down the road our daughter phones to tell us she's marrying a man neither of us has ever met before, you can bet I'll have a background check done on him, too."

"You know what this means, don't you?" she said, and bit into her lower lip. "We aren't going to have much of a honeymoon."

James chuckled. "Wanna bet?"

Summer grinned.

Whatever it was about this woman's smile should be bottled, James decided. It was the most potent aphrodisiac he'd ever encountered. He couldn't look at Summer and not want to make love to her.

"What about Julie?" James said in an effort to get Summer's mind off her parents' imminent arrival.

"Oh my, I nearly forgot my best friend." She reached for the phone and dialed Julie's number.

Being that there were several items that needed to be considered before the actual wedding ceremony, James walked over to the desk and sat down to write out a list, not wanting to chance forgetting something.

He was only half listening to the conversation between Summer and her roommate when he heard Summer's soft gasp and the mention of Jason, the man she'd once loved. James's ears perked up, and his fingers tightened around the writing instrument.

"What did you tell him?" Summer asked in low tones. This was followed by "Good. Then you're coming? Great. You might want to talk to my parents and see if you can fly in with them. I'm sure they're eager to pump you for what you can tell them about James." After a few words of farewell, Summer replaced the receiver.

James turned around in his chair, wondering if Summer would volunteer the information about Jason.

"Julie's flying in, as well. I suggested she catch the same flight as my parents." She seemed self-conscious all at once.

Her eyes avoided his.

"So I heard." James waited, not wanting to approach the subject of her ex-fiancé, hoping she'd save him the trouble.

After an awkward moment, she blurted out, "Julie . . . Julie said Jason phoned."

James relaxed, grateful she chose not to hide it from him. "Did she find out what he wanted?"

"No. She hung up the phone on him before he got a chance to say."

James had the distinct feeling he was going to like Summer's roommate.

Summer's shoulders moved with an expressive sigh. "I don't think either of us is going to be nearly as happy once our family arrives."

"What makes you say that?" All he cared about, all that was important, was making Summer his wife.

"My mother's going to insist that we follow tradition and that we don't see each other all day."

James frowned. He wasn't keen on that idea.

"My dad will keep you occupied with a variety of questions. If you've got the slightest blemish on your record, he'll find out about it."

"I don't. Trust me, sweetheart, my background has been scrutinized by the very best. Your father isn't going to find anything the least bit unsavory."

She laughed softly. "In which case Dad will probably repeatedly thank you for taking me off his hands."

James grinned. He didn't know why the entire room remained between them. Then again, he did know. It would be damn easy to throw caution to the wind and make love to her right then and there. James felt as if he'd been waiting all his life for Summer Lawton. Now that he'd found her, even a minute longer seemed too much to ask.

From somewhere deep inside him, James would find the strength to resist her for one more night. But that was the limit of his endurance. The very limit.

Summer's parents arrived bright and early the following morning with Julie in tow. By chance Summer met them in the lobby on her way down for breakfast. James had phoned her room earlier, before she was dressed, to tell her he was headed for the coffee shop. Summer was too nervous to eat then, but since had developed a healthy appetite. She'd need fortification in order to deal with her parents.

"Mom. Dad. Julie."

They threw their arms around her as if the separation had been ten years instead of a few days.

"I called Adam and told him his little sister was getting married," were the first words out of her mother's mouth. "He's taking off work and he and Denise are driving in for the wedding."

"Mom," Summer protested, "James and I are having another ceremony later."

"Fine," Helen Lawton said without emotion, "Adam will be there, too. Now, stop fussing. It isn't like I held a gun to his head and told him he had to come. Your brother wants to be here."

"Daddy." Summer hugged her father. Stepping back, she placed her hands on her hips. "James is squeaky-clean, right?"

"How'd you know I had him checked?"

"You're my father, aren't you?" She slipped her arm around his waist and squeezed.

"How'd you ever meet a man like this?" Hank Lawton wanted to know. "He's good as gold."

"Yes, I know. I'm crazy about him."

James appeared then, coming from the direction of the coffee shop, a newspaper tucked under his arm.

Summer made the introductions, and while her family checked into their hotel rooms, Summer and James reserved a table in the coffee shop. They sat next to each other holding hands.

"Are you ready for all this?" he asked her.

"I don't know," she admitted. "My brother's taking the day off and driving in for the ceremony. I thought we'd have a small, intimate wedding."

"It's small and intimate."

"My brother and his wife have three small children, who will probably cry through the entire ceremony."

"I don't mind if you don't," James said, and gently squeezed her hand. "I suspect folks will talk about us the same way when we drag our children to family get-togethers."

"Our children," Summer repeated. Her heart went soft just thinking about having a family with James. "I'm eager for everything our life together holds. I'm looking forward to being a mother."

"Not nearly as eager as I am to make you one." The teasing light left his eyes. "If you have no objections, I'd like a large family. The number of children is up to you, but I'd like to suggest four."

"Four," she repeated, and nodded. "We're going to have a good life, James. I can feel it in my heart. We're going to be so happy."

"I feel that way, too. Being an only child, I was drawn to large families. I suspect that's the reason I've been such good friends with the Mannings over the years."

"Christy's family?"

He nodded. "She's the youngest of five."

Her parents appeared just then, and ever the gentleman, James stood until the ladies were seated.

"I hope you don't mind if we steal Summer away from you for the day," Helen said even before she looked at the menu. "We have a million and one things to do before the wedding."

"We do?" Summer didn't know why she bothered to protest. She'd known from the moment her parents announced they were coming that this would happen.

"First off, we're going to need to buy you a dress."

Silly as it seemed, Summer hadn't given much thought to her attire. A nice suit would do, she suspected, something flattering and stylish. The elaborate gown and veil would wait for the April ceremony.

"Then there's the matter of finding a preacher."

"The hotel provides a justice of the peace," James explained.

"Do you object to a man of the cloth?" Hank asked.

Summer wanted to leap to her feet and announce to James that this was a test, but she bit her tongue. Sooner or later her loving soon-to-be husband would learn to sink or swim on his own with her family.

"None. I'd prefer one myself."

Summer had to restrain herself from cheering. James had passed with flying colors.

"I've got the names of several ministers from our pastor in L.A.," her father announced. "We'll leave the women to do their thing, and you and I can find us a proper preacher." He said it in such a way that let it be known his little girl wasn't being married by any justice of the peace.

"What about rings?" Helen asked.

"I thought I'd pick up a couple of plain gold bands for now," James explained. "I'd like Summer to wear my mother's diamond. She can choose the setting at a later date, and it'll be ready before the April ceremony."

Breakfast wasn't the ordeal Summer had anticipated. Julie sent her curious looks now and again, and
Summer knew her friend was waiting for an opportune moment when they were alone so they could talk.

"We'll meet again at what time?" Helen asked, and
checked her watch.

Summer's father studied his own, while Summer
and James gazed longingly toward each other.

"Six," Helen suggested.

"That late?" Summer protested. They were being
cheated out of one entire day. No one seemed to appreciate that her time with James was already limited.

"I'll see to everything," her mother assured everyone in general. "Hank, all you need do is get James to
the chapel on time."

"There won't be any problem with my not showing." Apparently James felt the need to assure her
family of this. "I'm deeply in love with your daughter."

Julie's elbow connected with Summer's ribs. "What
did I tell you?" she whispered from the corner of her
mouth.

Julie had more than gloating on her mind, and so
did Summer's mother. At the first opportunity Helen
took them shopping. From the way she talked, a suit-
able wedding dress wasn't the only thing on her list. If
her daughter was about to marry a superior court
judge, then Summer would go to him with a complete
trousseau.

The minute Summer and Julie were alone in the
store, her roommate gripped hold of Summer's arm.
"I heard from Jason again," she whispered breathlessly.

"Again?"

"Yes. This time he stopped by the apartment, right before I left for the airport."

"No." Summer closed her eyes, not because she had any regrets when it came to her former fiancé. Nor did she harbor any doubts that she wasn't doing the right thing by marrying James.

It was as if Jason possessed some kind of radar and anticipated when he could cause her the most trouble.

"He's been asking around about you. Apparently he talked with a couple of the cast members at Disneyland. Steve and Sally? Do those names sound familiar?"

"Yes." Summer clenched her hands into tight fists. "I can't tell you how much this irritates me."

"You? The man's been making a first-class pest of himself all week. According to Jason, you're pining away for want of him."

"Oh, puhleese."

"That's what I told him."

"If I was pining for anyone," Summer said, "it was for James."

"Exactly. I told Jason that, too."

"Good."

"I explained with a good deal of satisfaction that you were involved with someone else now, and that he should stay out of your life."

"Good grief, he's married and about to become a father. The man has no principles." The thought of Jason looking to reestablish their relationship while his wife was pregnant with their child made Summer sick to her stomach. "I'm glad to be rid of him."

"You couldn't be getting married at a more opportune time. I'm telling you, Summer, from the way Jason argued with me, your marrying is about the only thing that will convince him it's over between the two of you.''

"You told him I was getting married, didn't you?''

"Yes, but he didn't believe me. He accused me of fabricating the whole thing. The man was downright insolent.''

"Girls, girls.'' Helen returned with a salesclerk.

"I wonder how long it will be before she considers us women?'' Summer asked her friend under her breath.

By evening Summer felt more like a French poodle than she did a bride. She'd been shampooed from head to foot, her nails had been polished, her hair curled, her body rubbed and oiled. She'd been in and out of more clothes than a New York fashion model. And she was exhausted.

The idea of a white chic suit for the wedding was one of the first ideas to go. Before Summer could argue, she was draped in satin and silk from head to toe.

"You look absolutely stunning,'' Helen insisted.

Summer wasn't sure she should trust her mother's assessment. Her eyes went to Julie.

"She's right.''

"But what about April?'' If they went to so much fuss now, none of the pomp would be saved for the larger ceremony in the spring.

"What about it?'' Helen's hands went into the air. "You'll wear the dress twice. Big deal. No one need know.''

"It's so much money.''

"My baby girl only gets married once.''

No matter how many times she said it, Summer couldn't make her family understand that in this case it was twice.

Julie arranged the veil and the long train for the photographer who was said to be on his way, then handed Summer the intricate gardenia bouquet. "If you're going to throw that, just be sure and aim it my way."

Summer smiled. "You got it."

"Not yet, I haven't," Julie reminded her.

A knock sounded against the door, and Helen saw to it. Summer didn't pay any attention, assuming it was the man her father had hired to take the pictures.

"Hello, hello," Helen greeted the tall, balding man enthusiastically. "Summer, this is James's father, Walter. You should have told me he was a retired superior court judge himself."

Summer would have been happy to, had she known.

"My oh my," Walter said as he entered the room. He stood in front of Summer, his hands braced against his hips, and he slowly shook his head. "Exactly where did my son ever meet such a beauty?"

"Here in Vegas," Summer answered. "A year ago."

"I was about to give up hope on that son of mine. It seemed to me he'd settled comfortably into bachelorhood. This comes as a most pleasant surprise."

"I'm very pleased you came to meet me and my family, especially on such short notice."

Walter withdrew a thick cigar from the inside of his suit pocket and examined the end of it. "I wouldn't have missed this for the world."

Walter sat down in a chair and made himself comfortable. After a moment he returned the cigar to his inside pocket. "I gave up smoking five years ago and by heaven I still miss it. Every now and again I take one out and look at it just for the thrill."

Summer could see that she was going to like James's father.

"To be frank, I didn't think that boy of mine possessed this much common sense."

"He's a judge," Summer said, eager to defend her husband-to-be.

"When it comes to the law, James is one of the finest men on the bench. He seems to be worried about the November election, but as far as I can see, he won't have a problem. What I'm talking about is something else entirely."

Summer felt like sitting down herself. Both her mother and Julie had mysteriously disappeared, and since the photographer had yet to show, she was going to relax.

"Have you seen James?" she asked, missing him dreadfully.

"Oh, yes."

"How is he?" She folded her hands, wondering what James was thinking and if he was sorry he'd ever gotten involved in all this. Everything had seemed so uncomplicated when they'd discussed it the day before.

"He's pacing."

"Pacing," she repeated, certain this was a bad sign.

"It's a good thing this wedding was scheduled less than an hour from now. I don't know that your father and brother could keep James away from you much longer than that."

Summer relaxed.

"The boy's downright smitten. Never thought I'd see the day he'd fall head over heels in love like this. It does my old heart good."

"But he was engaged. I know about Christy Manning."

"Ah, yes, Christy. She was a dear girl, and James did have strong feelings for her, but deep down I believe what he found so attractive about Christy was her family. There's quite a difference between the love James has for you and what he felt for Christy Manning. As you'll recall, he was content to stay engaged for a good long while. My heavens, he's marrying you so fast, my head's spinning. His is, too, from the looks of him. You've thrown him for quite a loop."

"I love James, too," Summer said with feeling, "very much."

"Good. I sincerely hope the two of you will seriously consider making me a grandfather soon. I'm filthy rich and looking for a grandchild or two to spoil."

"We've decided on four."

"Four." Walter looked downright pleased. "But you're worried."

"Yes," she said softly, wondering how he knew. "My biggest fear is that I'm not the right kind of wife for James. I'm afraid I might inadvertently do something to harm his career."

"What makes you think that?"

"I'm an actress, remember?"

"Ah, yes, and that's worrying you?"

"I have this tendency to speak what's on my mind."

"Frankly I find that refreshing."

"You will until I put my foot in my mouth and embarrass the entire family. To give you an example . . ."

She hesitated, wondering if she should continue, then realized she couldn't very well stop now. "It was me who suggested to James that the two of us marry."

"Really?"

"It just came out. It seemed like a brilliant idea at the time . . . you know how good things can sound until you've thought them through. Well, anyway James looked at me like he'd swallowed his tongue."

Walter burst out laughing. "Forgive me, my dear, continue, please."

"Naturally I felt like a first-class fool. Mainly because James didn't say anything and didn't say anything and didn't say anything, and I was convinced I'd ruined everything."

"He said nothing, did he?"

"Well, he did mumble something about preferring to do the asking himself, which is completely understandable."

"And you clammed up."

"Oh, quite the opposite. I started talking at hurricane-force speed until he very gently told me it was fine and I needn't worry. An eternity later, after I'd fallen all over myself telling him how sorry I was, he said he thought it was a good idea. James was the one who came up with the idea of a ceremony now and then one later in April."

"James did?" Clearly this was news to his father.

"Yes." Summer grinned sheepishly. "He said something along the line of impulsive suggestions being contagious."

"My goodness, there's more to the boy than I assumed."

A knock sounded against the door, and a man with a camera let himself inside.

"You must be the photographer," Summer said, and stood.

"I'd better get back to James," Walter announced. "It's been a pure delight meeting you, Summer. I don't have a shred of doubt that you're the best thing to come along in my son's life in a very long time. Make him happy, Summer, make him very happy."

"I intend to do my best."

"And while you're at it, teach him how to laugh."

Summer nodded. "I will." She had a sneaky suspicion they were going to teach one another everything they needed to know about life.

James looked at his watch for the third time that minute. No one seemed to understand that he needed to see Summer. Needed to talk to her, find out about her day and tell her about his. Frustration ate at him like battery acid.

If he'd had so much of an inkling that their wedding was going to cause such a big hullabaloo, he would never have agreed to contact their families.

James liked Summer's parents, but frankly he'd prefer to spend his time with her.

"We can go into the chapel now," Hank Lawton announced.

James was so grateful he felt like cheering. According to his calculations, the ceremony would take approximately twenty minutes, thirty at the most. They'd sign the marriage certificate afterward, and the rest of the time was theirs alone. He wouldn't tolerate any more of these separations, however brief. The next time Summer left his sight, it would be at the airport.

The small chapel was filled with guests, and the organ music burst through the enclosed room like an announcer calling the first baseball pitch of the season.

James stood in front with the minister, Reverend Floyd Wilson. James had rented the tuxedo because it seemed something of an oddity for the father of the bride to be in one and not the groom. Now, however, the shirt seemed too tight around the collar. He resisted the urge to insert his finger and give himself a little extra breathing space.

It was then that Summer appeared.

James felt as if someone had knocked him in the knees with a bat. Never in all his life had he seen anyone more beautiful. His heart beat so hard and fast that it felt as though it was about to come straight through his chest.

Her dress was silk and lace with pearls, as traditional a wedding gown as any he'd seen. One would think Summer were a debutante and this were a society wedding.

When she joined him at the altar and placed her arm in his, James felt this was the proudest moment of his life. He knew that a few months in the future they'd repeat this ceremony, but nothing would match the incredible blend of humility and pride he experienced right then.

The ceremony itself was a blur to him. James's full concentration was on the woman at his side. He knew she was feeling some of the same emotion when she went to repeat her vows.

Summer's voice shook slightly, and it sounded as if she were close to tears. His arm tightened around hers. James felt like weeping himself. With gratitude, with wonder that this beautiful, vibrant woman would marry a stuffed-shirt bachelor like him.

"I now pronounce you husband and wife. You may kiss your bride."

James didn't need to be urged a second time. Carefully he gathered Summer in his arms. He sighed when their lips met in the tenderest, sweetest kiss of his life.

She clung to him. "Oh, James, how soon can we get rid of everyone?"

He'd entertained that very question from the moment Summer's mother had taken her from him that morning.

"Soon," he promised. Only heaven knew how they were going to manage being separated for the next four months.

They were hit with a barrage of birdseed on their way out the door. They laughed and tried to catch it in their outstretched hands.

"Pictures," Helen insisted, and when Summer groaned, she added, "Just a few more, and that's all."

"Mother, you'll get plenty of pictures later."

"I want some now," her mother insisted.

By the time they finished, James suspected there was going to be a permanent yellow dot in front of his eyes.

They signed the marriage license, and thinking no one was watching, James took the opportunity to kiss her. "I don't ever want to spend another day like this one," he whispered.

"Me, either," she said, then giggled. "It wasn't all for naught. Mother insisted on buying me this darling little black nightie."

James could feel the hot blood circle his ears and... other places. "Your mother bought you a nightie?"

"She said that me in that black slip of nothing was her wedding gift to you."

"I'll thank her later."

"Wait until you see what Julie got us," she whispered.

James's throat felt thick, but again that wasn't the only place in his body that experienced the stiffening sensation. "I have the feeling it isn't a toaster."

"No. She picked it out when Mom wasn't looking. You do like tassels, don't you?"

"Tassels?"

"Shh." Summer looked around to be sure no one was listening. "I'll save them for after the honeymoon."

"Why?"

"Because, my darling husband, they cover the best part, and I—" She stopped abruptly.

"Yes?" he coaxed.

"Husband," she said the word as if she were saying a prayer. "James, you're my husband."

"I know, wife." It hit him then, too, the way it had her, he suspected. The beauty of it, of belonging to each other, of the word itself.

Their families returned all at once. Adam was there with Denise and the three children. James was introduced to them again, although he'd met them before the ceremony.

"I don't know about anyone else," Helen Lawton said, "but I'm starved."

A chorus of agreement rose.

"We'll say good-night, then," James announced. "Thank you all for making this the most incredible day of my life."

"It's early yet," Helen protested.

"Helen," Hank snapped. "Think about it."

"Oh, yes, sorry." Helen's face brightened, and she smiled apologetically to James.

"Will we see you in the morning?"

"Helen?"

"I'm just asking, Hank. What harm is there in asking?"

"I don't know, Mom. What time is your flight out?"

James didn't listen to the answer, although he supposed he should have. As it was, he was having a hell of a time hiding his impatience. All the time he had left with his wife...his wife—his wife—his mind mulled over the word once more—was two days. Luckily that was two days and *three* nights. From what he understood, their flights left within a half hour of each other, and then it would be one entire month before he could see Summer again.

"All right, then, darling," Helen said, hugging Summer, "we'll see you both in the morning."

The entourage left, and James was alone with Summer at last.

"Are we going to my room or yours?" she asked, smiling up at him.

"Neither. I rented the honeymoon suite here for the night. Your mother packed your suitcase and had it sent over."

"You think of everything." She reached up and removed the wedding veil and shook her head, freeing her curls. "I can't tell you how anxious I am to get out of this dress."

James chuckled as he led the way to the elevator. "Not nearly as anxious as I am to get you out of it."

"Who were all those guests?" she asked him when they stepped inside the elevator car.

"I thought they were friends of yours."

"I've never seen them before in my life."

James shrugged. "Me, either."

"You know what? I bet my mother invited them to attend the wedding. She couldn't bear to have us married in an empty chapel."

James fingered the room key in the palm of his hand. "Are you hungry?"

"No."

"Good, because I thought we'd work up an appetite."

Summer smiled and moistened her lips with the tip of her tongue. "I have a curious feeling you aren't talking about racquetball, either."

James cleared his throat. He wanted her so much his body trembled with the strength of his need. "You could be right about that."

Chapter Six

James amazed Summer. She wasn't sure what she expected from him as a lover, but it wasn't this. They'd made love no less than three times during their wedding night, and Summer woke the following morning to find him standing at the foot of their bed, fresh from the shower.

His nude body glistened in the early-morning light. Droplets of water dripped from his hair and onto the mat of dark curls that covered his chest.

"Good morning, Mrs. Wilkens."

Summer smiled and stretched her arms high above her head, arching her back. The sheet slipped away, exposing her bare breasts.

"Good morning, husband." She noticed he was fully aroused and slowly lifted her gaze to his. Already her body was responding to him, throbbing with readiness and need. James's eyes narrowed as they focused on her breasts.

Wordlessly she knelt up on the bed and held her arms out to him. She smiled to herself, thinking someone should have warned her about this man before they married. At this rate, she estimated they'd both be dead inside a week.

He walked over to the side of the mattress, kissed her once, twice and then placed his knee on the edge of the bed, as if he needed its support to remain upright.

In all her life Summer had never experienced such power. Or such love. He placed his hands on her breasts and lifted them. The thumbs grazed the centers, and her nipples peaked and hardened. A mere brush of his hand, and they stood at attention, arousing her.

Summer went still, her breathing slow and shallow. She half closed her eyes at the pleasure the simple touch of his hand wrought.

James groaned, and Summer had come to recognize the meaning. He couldn't wait any longer. Neither could she. She looped her arms around his neck and slowly lay back against the mattress, bringing him with her.

James braced his hands on either side of her hips, shifted her and carefully guided himself into her.

Summer shuddered and went stock-still as he eased his way into her, burying himself to the hilt. It was better than before. Each time the pleasure increased until it was more than she could bear. More joy than she could manage to keep to herself.

Waves of pleasure radiated through her, and she lifted her buttocks in an effort to work her body against his, to accommodate the full length of his thick staff more completely.

Her small movement caused them both to gasp.

"Summer, don't move," he warned between clenched teeth.

"I can't help it. You feel so good."

"That's the problem. You do, too."

She smiled contentedly at the warm touch of her husband, buried deep inside her. All at once her eyes flew open. "James, you forgot..."

"It'll be all right," he assured her as he began to move. "Just this one time."

She wasn't eager to have him stop. Not now. "Okay." She arched her back and held on tight as he began moving strongly, setting a steady pace and rhythm.

Eagerly Summer accepted his thrusts, meeting each one. She cradled his sex, the inner muscles of her womanhood clasping him. Summer could feel the approach of her completion and whimpered, wildly rocking her body against her husband's.

James reached his climax seconds after she experienced her own. A harsh groan tore from his throat, and his powerful body shuddered.

His shoulders continued to heave as he gathered her in his arms and spread soft, delicate kisses over her face. He went to move from her, but she tightened her legs around his waist and wouldn't let him.

"Not yet," she pleaded. "I want to be a part of you."

"You are. You always will be. You could travel to Mars, and my heart would be with you." He brushed the hair from her face. "I can't believe you love me."

"I do so much my heart feels like it's about to burst wide open. Will it always be like this?" she asked. "Two weeks ago you were someone whose kind letters I looked forward to receiving. This week you're the most important person in my life."

James kissed the tip of her nose. "I have the feeling it only gets better from here on out."

"Better?" She couldn't believe it. Didn't know if that were humanly possible. "I can't imagine it."

In one uninterrupted movement James rolled onto his back, taking her with him so that she was sprawled across his chest. Across his heart. "I can't, either. Dear, sweet heaven, I love you."

"Good." She pressed her head against his shoulder.

"I'll remember next time," he promised. "The last thing we need now is an unplanned pregnancy."

"I'm pretty sure this is my safe time, don't worry."

James kissed her neck. "I suppose we should get dressed and meet your family."

"I suppose," she agreed, but neither of them showed any signs of wanting to move.

"It won't be so bad," James whispered.

They'd been married less than twenty-four hours and already Summer could read her husband's thoughts. "Being separated? It's going to be hell on earth. I don't know how I'll last four months without you."

"Four months." He made the two words sound like an eternity. That was the way they felt just then.

"James, I know this sounds a little ridiculous, seeing that I'm your wife and all, but where do you live?"

His brow folded in question. "Seattle."

"I know that, silly, but in an apartment? A condo? A town house or what?"

"A house."

Summer liked the idea of that.

A slow grin spread across his face. "I must have known I was going to meet you. This is a very big house on Queen Anne Hill with seven bedrooms."

"James!"

"It's a lovely older home. I'm quite proud of the gardens. I hope you'll like it."

"I love it already."

"You haven't seen it."

"No, but I saw the look that came into your eyes when you spoke of it. It's going to be perfect for us, just perfect."

His eyes grew dark and serious. "You're perfect."

"I hope we'll always love each other as much as we do this moment." Summer pressed her head to his chest and sighed.

Time had never passed more quickly for James. He dreaded he would have to leave Summer almost from the moment they'd met again on New Year's Eve. It was as though Seattle were another world, another time, and frankly he wasn't that eager to return to the life that awaited him. Not when it meant having to say goodbye to Summer.

His wife of two days had been unusually quiet when they packed their suitcases the morning of their scheduled departure. When she found him watching her, she'd offered him a reassuring smile.

The bellboy carted their luggage to the lobby at the Four Queens. While James was checking out of the hotel, he noticed Summer twisting the plain gold band around her finger. His own felt awkward and heavy on his finger, and he wondered if she were experiencing any regrets. For his own part, he didn't harbor a single one.

Having dispensed with the rental car earlier, James ordered a taxi. He held hands with Summer as they silently rode to the airport.

He wanted to assure her it wouldn't be so bad, but that would have been a bold-faced lie. Every minute he was away from her was too much. He wanted to be sure she understood how much he loved her, how important she was to him. But the back seat of a taxi didn't seem to be the appropriate place to tell one's wife those things.

Nothing would ever be the same for either of them again, and they both knew it. That was the problem.

The taxi dropped them off, and James paid the tab. Since they were flying on different airlines, they separated to check in their luggage and receive their seat assignments.

James finished first and caught sight of Summer weaving her way through the crowd. Even from the distance he sensed her sadness. He met her halfway.

"I'm on Concourse B," she said, looking down at her ticket. Her voice was small and tight.

"Concourse A."

"What time do you leave?"

She already knew, but apparently needed to hear it one last time. "Ten-thirty," James told her.

"I'm scheduled to depart at ten."

He was perfectly aware of what time her plane left. "I'll walk down to Concourse B with you."

"You can't, James, you might miss your own flight."

Frankly he didn't give a damn. "Then I'll catch the next one."

"I'll worry. James, really, I'm a big girl. I can find my way around an airport."

"I didn't say you couldn't," he snapped back, surprising himself with the vehemence with which he spoke.

Summer looked up at him with eyes brimming with tears. She turned and walked away from him and headed for Concourse B.

James followed and wanted to kick himself. He didn't know how long it would be before he could see his wife again and he appeared to be doing his utmost to start an argument with her. No doubt there was some deep psychological meaning to his attitude. Damn but this was difficult. He'd examine what was happening later, but at the moment he was more concerned about having to say goodbye to his wife.

Summer arrived at the appropriate gate and walked over to the window. James could see her plane and knew it wouldn't be more than a few moments before the boarding call was announced.

"I'm sorry, sweetheart." He braced his hands against her shoulders and closed his eyes, feeling the need to reel in his emotions.

"Me, too."

He frowned. She'd done nothing wrong. "For what?"

"Oh, James," she whispered brokenly, and slipped her arms around his waist. "I'm going to be so lost without you."

"It's going to be hell." He wasn't willing to pretend otherwise. "I'll phone as often as I can."

"Do you have my work schedule?"

"Yes. Do you have everything you need?" They'd gone over the details a dozen times or more.

"No. I need you, James."

His hold on her tightened. He wondered if they were afraid they'd lose the magic. Afraid that once they flew back to their respective lives, all would be lost.

Her flight number was announced, and James's heart clenched. It wouldn't be long, he promised himself. A week, two at the outside. A few moments later her row assignment was called to board.

"That's you," he breathed reluctantly.

"I know."

But neither of them made a move to break apart.

Summer was the last one to board the plane, and James was left to tear through the airport in order to catch his own flight. If anyone had suggested as little as ten days ago that the dignified James Wilkens would race through an airport in order to spend a few extra minutes with a woman, he would have scoffed. He wasn't scoffing now. He would have done a whole lot more than race if it would have kept Summer with him longer.

He arrived in the nick of time and collapsed into his plane seat, his heart racing.

Between dashing through airports and making love, he was convinced Summer would be the death of him yet. He smiled as he snapped his seat belt into place. If he was to die right at that moment, he mused, he'd leave this earth a happy man.

James's house had never seemed more empty. By the time he arrived, it was dark and shadow filled. His first mistake had been stopping off at the office on his way back from the airport. After he arrived in Seattle, he'd spent what remained of the day working through the phone memos, briefs and reading over case histories. He was willing to do anything in order to arrange time away as soon as possible.

It didn't take long for him to push aside the memories of the incredible week in Vegas or the woman he'd married and return to the life that awaited him. Summer, however, was never far from his thoughts.

By the time he arrived home, suitcase in hand, he was dragging. He switched on the light in the kitchen and set his briefcase down on the walnut table in the breakfast nook.

He hadn't eaten anything since that morning, and a look inside the refrigerator reminded him he'd been away all week. He'd need to order out or defrost something from the freezer.

Deciding against both, he heated a can of soup, ate, then showered. He'd showered that morning, but Summer had been in the stall with him and neither one of them had seemed particularly concerned about washing.

James stood in front of the bathroom mirror. He smeared shaving cream over his face and stared back at the reflection that greeted him. He didn't look all that different than the man he was a week ago. But he was different.

Unable to delay talking to Summer, he wiped the shaving cream from his face with a hand towel and headed for his book-lined den.

Having memorized her phone number when she'd first given it to him, James dialed it by heart.

Summer answered on the first ring, as if she were just as eager to hear from him. "Hello."

"Hello, darling."

"Hello, James."

"I would have phoned sooner, but I went to the office. I needed to clear off my desk."

"Did you check your calendar?"

"First thing. I can fly down on a Saturday morning in two weeks, but I'll need to be back Sunday afternoon. That doesn't give us much time."

"No," she agreed, "but we'll make the most of it." Her relief was evident. "I was afraid once you looked over your schedule you'd find it impossible to get away."

"I don't care what it takes, I'll be in California in two weeks."

"Wonderful. I traded weekends with a friend so I can be with you in February. My mother's already started work on the wedding. She's called and left a message with the secretary at the Moose Hall. It's really a very nice building."

"Your mother's enjoying every minute of this, isn't she?"

Summer giggled. "Yes. But the one who surprises me the most is my dad. I don't know what you said or did, but my dad thinks you walk on water."

"It can be arranged."

"That's what I thought."

Quiet butted against quiet. They'd spent nearly every minute of the previous week together. They'd discussed everything there was to discuss. Yet neither was willing to break the connection.

An hour later James decided this was probably a stage most young men go through at some point in their teen years. He'd spent the better part of an hour on the phone with Summer, and they hadn't spoken more than an occasional word between whispered promises and deep sighs. They'd shared secrets, mostly about each other, and done a lot of heavy breathing. In essence they'd ended up making love to each other long-distance.

When it was over, however, James was feeling a whole lot worse physically than he had before he phoned. Their next conversation, he'd let Summer know he wasn't up to much more of that.

"I've gotten together with a group of businessmen and spread the word," Ralph Southworth was saying.

James sat in his office and gazed into the distance. As always his thoughts were fifteen hundred miles to the south with Summer. He barely heard his campaign manager. In eight days he'd be with Summer. The last six had been the purest form of torture.

He lived for the time he could phone her. Because she performed in the last show of the night, he couldn't reach her until after ten, and more often than not they spoke until past midnight. James didn't want to think about his phone bill. Not that it mattered; he would have gladly paid ten times whatever the long-distance fee was for the opportunity to talk to his wife.

"There's a dinner party this Friday night at the Morrisons," Ralph announced.

James didn't comment.

"You're going, aren't you?"

"To the Morrisons'?"

Ralph Southworth looked at him as if he expected to see something dangling from the end of James's nose. "Who else do you think I mean?"

James shrugged. Ralph was a good man, a bit abrasive at times, but sincere and hardworking. Ac-

cording to people James trusted, Ralph Southworth
was the best man for the job of getting James elected
to the superior court.

"What's with you lately, James?" Ralph asked
abruptly. He pulled out a chair and plunked himself
down across from James's desk.

Ralph was nothing if not direct. "What makes you
ask?"

"Something's not right. Ever since you got back
from vacation, you haven't been the same."

James weighed telling Ralph the truth. A part of
him was eager to share the news of his marriage.
Marrying Summer was nothing to be ashamed of, but
the arrangements for the second ceremony were being
made for their wedding in April. If he were willing to
face the truth, James wasn't keen on explaining his
sudden marriage to the man who'd frowned upon
James vacationing in Vegas. He preferred to leave
matters as they were and invite Ralph to the wedding
in April and leave it at that.

"Have you ever been in love?" James asked.

Ralph adamantly shook his head. "Never, and
proud of it."

James's eyebrows shot to his hairline. "I see."

"Women have ruined more than one good man.
Don't be a fool, James, and do something stupid at
this point. Unless it's someone that can help you politically, of course. Now, if you were to announce
you'd fallen for Mary Horton . . ."

"Who?"

"Mary Horton . . . never mind, she's not your type.
All I can say is that if you're going to get involved
now, just be sure it's with someone who can help you
politically."

"She can't."

Ralph tossed his hands into the air. "Somehow or other I knew you were going to say that. For the love of heaven, keep your head screwed on tight and your pants zipped. The last thing we need now is a scandal, understand?"

"Of course. Summer's not like..."

"Her name is Summer?" Ralph rolled his eyes expressively. "James, listen to me. You've asked me to head up your campaign, and I'm pleased to do it, but I'm telling you right now, getting involved with a woman named Summer is another word for trouble."

"Don't you think you're being unnecessarily unfair?"

"No. Where'd you meet her?"

"Vegas."

Ralph's mouth thinned. "Don't tell me she's a show girl," he ordered.

"No, but she's an actress."

A muscle leapt in his friend's jaw. "Don't say anything more. Not a single word, understand? I've already got high blood pressure and I have the feeling I don't want to know more than what you've already told me."

"Summer has nothing to do with you," James said, having a difficult time quelling his irritation. Ralph made Summer sound like the worst thing that had ever happened to him.

"I don't suppose you remember a certain congressman who got involved with a stripper a few years back."

"Summer isn't a stripper."

"It ruined him, James. Ruined him. I don't want the same thing to happen to you."

"It won't. Furthermore, I won't have you speaking about her in those tones." In light of Ralph's reaction, James didn't think now was the time to announce they were already married. "If you must know, I intend to marry her."

"Great, do it after the election."

"We've decided on April."

"April," Ralph barked. "That's much too soon. Listen, you're paying me big money to run this campaign. You want my advice, you've got it. What difference does a few months make?" He paused and waited for James's reaction. "Will you do that one thing?"

"I don't know."

"Are you afraid you'll lose her?"

"No," James returned adamantly.

"Then put off the wedding until after the election. Is it so much to ask?"

"I don't know which is worse," Julie said, running the bright red polish over her toenail, "this year or last."

"What do you mean?" Summer asked.

"You." She swirled the brush in the red paint and started with the little toe on her left foot. "Last year, after you broke up with Jason, you moped around the apartment all despondent and glum."

Summer laughed. "This year isn't much better, is it?"

"Not that I can see. Listen, I understand how much you miss James. The guy's a hunk. It isn't any wonder you fell in love with him. If the situation was reversed, you can bet I'd be just as miserable. The thing is, you won't be apart for long. April's right around the corner. It's obvious the guy's crazy about you, too. It could be worse."

Summer folded her arms and leaned against the back of the sofa. "I didn't know it was possible to love someone as much as I do James. I miss him so much."

"If the number of times he phones you is any indication, then I'd say he feels the same way."

"He works so hard." Summer knew that many of James's late-night calls originated from his office. She also knew that he was putting in extra long hours in order to free up time so he could spend them with her.

"He'll be here in a matter of days."

"I know."

"You haven't told him about Jason?" Julie wanted to know.

Summer's nails bit into the palms of her hands. "What good would it do? James is fifteen hundred miles away. Jason hasn't got a chance with me. Unfortunately he just doesn't seem ready to accept that. If he repeatedly gets the same message, then he might learn."

"By the way, when James visits, I'm out of here."

"Julie, you don't need to leave. We can get a hotel room—really, we don't mind."

"Don't be ridiculous. This is your home. You'd be more relaxed here, and both of you have been through enough stress lately."

Summer was so grateful it was all she could do not to weep. It was the stress, she decided, this tendency to be overly emotional. "Have I told you how glad I am you're my friend?"

"Think nothing of it."

"I mean it, Julie. I don't know what I would have done without you these last couple of weeks. I feel like my whole world's been turned upside down."

"It has been. I don't know anyone else who goes away for a week and returns married. Did you think James had gone nuts when he suggested it?"

"Yes," she admitted, remembering the most fabulous dinner of her life. "A little. I don't think James has done anything impulsive in his entire life."

Julie grinned. "That is until he met you."

"Funny, James made the same comment."

The phone pealed just then, and Summer leapt up to answer it on the off chance it was James.

"Hello," she said breathlessly.

"Summer, don't hang up, please, I'm begging you."

"Jason." Her heart sank. "Please," she told him, "just leave me alone."

"Talk to me. That's all I'm asking."

"About what? We have absolutely nothing to say to each other."

"I made a mistake."

Summer closed her eyes, fighting back the frustration. "It's too late. What do I have to say to convince you of that. You're married, I'm married."

"I don't believe it." His voice tightened. "If you're married, then where's your husband?"

"I don't owe you any explanations. Don't phone me again. It's over and has been for a very long time."

"Summer, please . . . please."

She didn't wait to hear any more. His persistence astonished her. It seemed when she'd found him with another woman that he was almost glad. He'd acted relieved to be out of the relationship. In retrospect, Summer realized that Jason had fallen out of love with her long before but hadn't the courage to say anything. She never understood what prompted his actions. Later, when he married, and she learned it wasn't the same woman she'd found him with in Vegas, she wondered about this man she thought she knew so well, and realized she didn't know him at all.

His behavior mystified her. After loving Jason for six years, she expected to feel something toward him, but all the feeling she could muster was pity. She wanted nothing to do with him. He'd made his choice and she'd made hers.

"Jason? Again?" Julie asked when Summer joined her in the living room.

Summer nodded. "I hope this is the last of it."

"Have you thought about having the phone number changed?"

"Yes. I think it might be a good idea."

Julie studied her for a moment. "Are you going to tell James the reason why?"

"No. It would only worry him, and there's nothing he can do so far away. Jason doesn't concern me."

"Maybe he should."

Summer arrived at the Orange County airport forty minutes before James's flight was due to arrive on the off chance his plane came in early. Every minute of their day and a half together was carefully planned.

The only negative for Summer was the brunch with her parents Sunday morning. Her mother had several concerns about planning the wedding that she needed to discuss with James. Summer begrudged every minute she had to share James, and realized she was being selfish, but she didn't care.

Julie, true to her word, had made a weekend trip to visit a longtime family member. An aunt in Claremont or somewhere near Ontario. Summer was eternally grateful.

By the time James's plane touched down, she was nearly sick to her stomach with anticipation. The Orange County airport was small enough not to use jet ways. As soon as James stepped out of the airplane, he paused and searched her out.

Their eyes connected and in that minisecond before he started down the steps, it felt as if someone had pushed a button in her heart.

When they'd parted in Las Vegas it felt as if everything had come to a sudden and abrupt standstill. Now she could see him, could feel him for the first time since they'd parted two weeks previously.

Weaving her way between those coming from the plane, she raced toward him. James caught her in his arms and crushed her against him. His hands were in her hair, and his mouth hungrily sought hers.

His embrace half lifted her from the ground. She clung to him, fighting back a flood of emotion. Unexpectedly tears filled her eyes, but she was too happy to care.

James broke off the kiss, and Summer stared up at him, smiling. Damn but it was good to see him.

"What's this?" he asked, brushing his thumb across the moisture wetting her cheeks.

"I don't know. I guess I missed you more than I realized."

"Damn but you're beautiful."

"I bet you tell all the women that," she joked.

"Nope, only the ones I marry."

Summer slipped her arm around his waist, and together they headed toward the luggage carousel. "I packed light."

"Good." Because it felt so good to be close to him, she stood on the tips of her toes and kissed his cheek. "You'll be pleased to hear Julie's gone for the weekend."

"Remind me to thank her."

"She's been great."

"Any more crank calls?"

Summer had almost forgotten that was the excuse she'd given him when she had had her phone number changed. "None." And then, because she was eager to change the subject, she told him, "I've got every minute planned."

"Every minute?"

"Well, almost. Mom and Dad invited us over for brunch in the morning. I couldn't think of any way to get out of it."

"That might be a good idea."

"Why?"

James frowned, and she noticed for the first time the dark circles under his eyes. He was working too hard, not sleeping enough. She didn't want to think about what he was doing for meals. That would all change when she arrived in Seattle. The first thing she was going to do was be sure he ate properly. As for time in bed, well, she didn't anticipate that would be a problem.

"There might be something of a problem," he said with heavy reluctance.

Summer stopped midstep, not sure how to translate his announcement.

"What does it matter, Summer? We're already married."

"I know, but..."

"We can talk about it later, with your family. All right?"

She nodded, unwilling to waste one precious moment arguing over something as silly as a fancy wedding when she already wore his ring.

"My apartment's less than fifteen minutes from the airport," she told him as he loaded his suitcase into the back of her small car. "There's a reason I'm telling you this."

"Yes?" He slipped into the passenger seat.

Summer started the engine and released the buttons of her sweater, exposing a thin white T-shirt beneath. She looked over and smiled beguilingly at her husband.

James groaned. "You're not wearing a bra, are you?"

Summer threw back her head and laughed. "What makes you think that?"

Chapter Seven

James was convinced Summer had gone braless with the sole purpose of slowly but surely driving him insane. He couldn't keep his eyes off her breasts. No matter how hard he tried. They tantalized him, teased and tempted him. The past two weeks without her had redefined the word *lonely*. Had redefined the concept of needing another person to the point of suffering actual physical pain.

For years James had lived an impassive and sober life-style. He'd never considered himself a carnal man. Three weeks after marrying Summer, making love occupied far more of his thoughts than it had in the previous thirty-odd years totaled.

"How far did you say it was to your apartment?" he asked.

Summer didn't immediately respond.

"Summer?"

"It seems to me we have a few things we need to discuss."

"All right," he said, forcing himself to remove his gaze from her front. The woman had him at a distinct disadvantage. Right then he would have agreed to just about anything no matter where the discussion led.

"I want to know what you meant about there being a problem with the wedding."

He should have known it had to do with that. "Sweetheart, it has more to do with your parents than you and me. Let's not spend time worrying about that now."

"You want to delay the wedding, don't you?"

"No," he responded vehemently. "Do you honestly think I'm enjoying this separation? I couldn't be any more miserable."

"Me, either."

"Then you have to believe that I wouldn't do anything that would mean we couldn't be together." Frankly James was worried about Summer. She seemed pale and drawn, as if she weren't sleeping well or eating right. The situation wasn't good for either one of them.

They didn't say anything more about the wedding date, and James was grateful, although they would need to discuss it at some point.

When they arrived at her apartment, he carried in his suitcase and set it down in the small living room. His gaze traveled about the compact rooms.

Summer's personality marked each area. The apartment was bright and cheerful. The kitchen strongly appealed to him, with bold yellow cabinets with red knobs. Without asking, he knew this was Summer's special touch.

She led him into her bedroom, and he stopped when his eye caught the five-foot wall poster of her as Beauty posing with the Beast. She was so damn beautiful he couldn't take his eyes off the mounted portrait. He felt a kernel of jealousy for the man who was able to spend time with her each night, even if it was dressed in costume.

His gaze moved from the picture to the bed. A single. He supposed it wouldn't matter. The way he felt just then, they'd spend the entire night making love anyway.

He turned toward his wife. She smiled softly, and in that instant James knew he couldn't wait any longer to make love to her. His need was so great that his entire body seemed to throb with a life of its own, a need of its own.

He held out his hand.

Summer lowered her gaze and slipped the cardigan from her arms. It fell to the floor and revealed a thin white T-shirt that did little to conceal her marvelous bounty. Her breasts were round and plump and seemed to proudly pout at him. Proudly seek his attention.

James never considered himself a breast man, but Summer had proved otherwise. His palms ached to touch her, and his lips hungered for a taste of her.

If he fostered any regrets about their time together in Vegas, it was that he'd been so eager for her, so awkward and clumsy that he'd came off like a Neanderthal. This time would be slow and easy, he'd promised himself. This time when they made love, it would be leisurely so she would know how much he appreciated her. Together they'd savor their love for each other.

"Summer, I love you." He lifted the shirt over her head and tossed it carelessly aside. Already his hands were at the snap of her denims, trembling as he struggled to hold back the urgency of his need.

He kissed her with two weeks' worth of pent-up hunger, and all his accumulated frustration broke free. His tongue searched out hers, and when she looped her arms around his neck and shyly met his movements with her own, James felt his knees start to give out on him.

He eased the fabric of jeans over her slender hips and let them fall to her feet. Her legs rubbed sensuously against his as she stepped out of the pants.

He released her long enough to remove his own bothersome clothes. As he was working his way out of his shirt and tie, he watched her slip out of her silky underwear. His breath froze, and his heart stopped abruptly. Soon it burst back to life again with a pulse that threatened to explode like thunder inside his chest.

James undressed in what he was sure was record time.

"Honey," he breathed, kissing her wildly.

"I know, I know."

They collapsed on the bed together. He kissed her deeply and with few other preliminaries, positioned himself above her and entered her. The wet, hot pleasure slid over him with fiery intensity. He groaned and, with his eyes closed and his teeth clenched, he eased forward, sinking deeper and deeper into her primitive heat.

Summer moaned, receiving him, taking in his strength, his power, his hardness and his love in one swift thrust. In that moment James was convinced he'd died and walked through the gates of paradise.

He paused only once, to allow her body to adjust to his. Then the fury began. It was as if James had been trapped in a wild storm. There was no pace, no rhythm. Only need, only fervor and intensity and a desire so strong it threatened to consume them both.

His need was raw and consuming, his hips pumping hers again and again. He felt swallowed up in the heat of their passion. Eagerly Summer met each push of his hips until his completion came, like all the New Year's Eve fireworks in one giant, cataclysmic release.

When it was over, all that could be heard was the broken cadence as James struggled to regain his breath. Unable to leave her, he rolled onto his side and looped his leg over her hip, maintaining the physical contact. Summer nestled in his arms and buried her face in his chest.

It didn't take James long to realize she'd fallen asleep. He didn't mind. Kissing the top of her head, he closed his eyes. So much for a leisurely time of lovemaking. So much for savoring each other. So much for going slow and easy.

He wished he understood what it was about this particular woman that drove him to the very brink of madness. Never had he loved anyone more completely. The way he craved her in the physical sense was as much a mystery to him as everything else.

Yet James wouldn't change as much as a hair on her head. He stroked her face and held her close. If he had his choice, he'd never let her go.

* * *

Summer woke to the sound of James humming off-key in the kitchen. It was clear the man couldn't carry a tune. Smiling, she reached for her housecoat and entered the kitchen to find him examining the contents of her refrigerator.

"So you're one of those," she teased, tying the sash of her robe as she joined him.

"One of what?" He reappeared with a chicken leg poised in front of his mouth.

"You get hungry after sex," she whispered.

"I didn't eat on the plane, and yes," he said, grinning almost shyly at her, "I suspect you're right."

She yawned and sat on the bar stool. "Find anything interesting in there for me?"

"Leftover chicken, cottage cheese three weeks past its expiration date, Swiss cheese and an orange."

"I'll take the orange." She yawned again.

"Have you been getting enough sleep?" He peeled the orange and frowned. It wasn't his imagination; she was pale.

"More than ever. I don't know what's wrong with me lately. All I do is work and sleep."

"Have you seen a doctor?"

"No. I'll be fine," she said, and forced herself to smile. She didn't want to waste their precious time together discussing her sleeping patterns. She glanced at her watch. "I better shower and get dressed."

"For the show?"

She nodded, saddened that part of her time with James would be spent on the job, but there was no help for it. It was difficult enough to trade weekends in order to fly up to Seattle.

"I'm anxious to discover what a talented woman I married."

"I hope I don't disappoint you."

"It isn't possible." His eyes were alight with love.

"James," she said, and bit into her lower lip. "Do you ever wonder about what's really between us?"

He tossed the chicken leg into the garbage. "What kind of question is that?"

"Sometimes I'm afraid that all we share is a strong physical attraction."

He swallowed, and the question seemed to make him uncomfortable. "What makes you ask that?"

"In case you haven't noticed, we can't keep our hands off each other. It's not just you. I'm guilty, too. I knew darn good and well when I dressed to pick you up this afternoon what would happen if I wore that T-shirt. I wanted it to happen.

"Having you want to make love to me so desperately heightens my own enjoyment. I think about us making love a lot...probably more than I should. You're a brilliant man. I'm fairly certain you didn't marry me because I challenge you intellectually."

"I married you because I fell in love with you."

He made it sound so uncomplicated.

"I love the way a room lights up when you walk into it," he said as if he needed to qualify the statement. "When you laugh, it makes me want to laugh, too. I've never heard you sing or seen you perform on stage, but there's music in you, Summer. I sensed it the first night we met.

"Just being with you makes me want to smile. Not that anything you say or do is especially funny. It's more an attitude. When I'm with you, I find the world is a better place to be."

Summer felt a knot tighten in her throat.

"Like your father, an attorney or a judge can get a jaded attitude toward life. It's difficult to trust when you find the world filled with suspicion. It's hard to love when you deal with the consequences of hate a good portion of each day. Perhaps that's been my problem all along."

"Not trusting?"

"Yes. You came to me without defenses, devastated, vulnerable, broken. I'd been hurt, too, so I knew how you felt because I'd experienced those identical emotions. I'd walk through the fires of hell before I'd allow anyone to do that to you again." He walked over and gave her the peeled orange. "I know it sounds like a bunch of words to say I love you, but it's true, Summer."

She gripped his hand with both of hers.

"If you believe our relationship is based on sexual attraction, then maybe we should put a hold on anything physical for the rest of the weekend. Instead, we'll concentrate on getting to know each other better." He dragged in a deep breath and held it as if it had cost him a good deal to make the offer.

"Do you think it's possible?" She gave him a knowing look, then leaned forward. The front of her robe gaped open, and Summer watched as her husband's gaze traveled to her bare breasts and stayed.

"It's possible," he said in a low, tight voice. "Not probable, but possible."

"I need to take a shower before I leave for work," she announced, and scooted off the stool. She started to walk away, then turned, looked over her shoulder and smiled seductively. "Remember what fun we had in the shower, James? We seemed to find some incredible uses for sudsy hands, didn't we?"

James paled. "Summer," he warned through clenched teeth. "If we're going to stay out of the bedroom, I'm going to need your help."

She turned to face him, hands akimbo. "The shower isn't in the bedroom."

"Go on," he said stiffly. "I'll wait for you here."

"You're sure?" She released the sash and let the silk robe fall open, exposing a large expanse of creamy white skin.

He made some sort of sound that could be translated either way. Feeling slightly disappointed, Summer walked into the bathroom and turned on the shower.

She hadn't done anything more than step inside and reach for the soap when the shower door was ripped open.

Naked, James stepped inside, and it was clear he was madder than blazes. "You know I can't resist you."

"Yes," she said softly, liberally lathering her hands.

"Then what the hell was all this talk about abstinence?"

Her hands found their destination, capturing his sex between her soap-slick fingers.

His eyes widened. "Summer, for the love of heaven . . . stop."

"Really?"

He leaned against the side of the shower, and his breathing became labored. "No," came the strangled reply. "I can't fight you, as well as myself."

"Good, because I don't want you to fight me."

"I can't," he whispered between bared teeth. "Now stop, before it's too late."

"I have no intentions of stopping until I get what I want."

"You little devil." He laughed and reached for the bar of soap. "You're going to pay for this."

"Promise?"

Summer and her mother were busy in the kitchen at the Lawton family home. James sat in the living room with his father-in-law, watching a football game between the Denver Broncos and the L.A. Raiders.

James hadn't the heart to explain to Hank that he didn't follow the sport all that much. If the truth be known, he found football boring.

"The wife's going to be talking to you later," Hank said, relaxing during a spell of uninterrupted beer commercials. "It seems she's having trouble getting a decent hall for the wedding reception in April. The church is no problem, mind you, but finding a hall has become one hell of a complication."

"Summer said something about the Moose Hall."

"That fell through. I'll let Helen do the explaining."

"Does Summer know this?"

"Not yet. Couldn't see upsetting her. The girl's been miserable ever since she returned from Vegas. You want my opinion?" He didn't wait for a response, eager to tell James exactly what he thought. "You should take her to Seattle with you now and be done with it. It's clear to me the two of you belong together. God knows she feels wretched without you."

James wished it were that easy.

"I know, I know," Hank said, scooting forward to the edge of the cushion as the football players ran back onto the muddy field at Mile High Stadium. "She's got to fulfill her contract. Never did understand where the girl got her singing talent."

"She's fabulous." Summer had shocked James with how good she was. Her performance as Belle had left him stunned.

Hank beamed proudly. "She's good, isn't she? I'll never forget the night I first went to see her perform at Disneyland. It was all I could do not to stand up and yell out that she was my little girl."

"There's such power in her voice."

"Enough to crack crystal, isn't it? One would never suspect it hearing her speak, but the minute she opens her mouth to sing, watch out. I've never heard anything like it."

James had come away awed by the magnitude of talent Summer possessed. That she would willingly walk away from her career to be his wife boggled his mind.

"She could go all the way to the top."

Hank nodded. "I think so, too, if she wanted, but that's the crux of it. She enjoys singing, don't get me wrong, but Summer will be just as happy humming lullabies to her babies as she would be performing in some hit Broadway show."

The area around James's heart tightened at the thought of Summer softly singing their children goodnight.

"Helen's mother used to sing," Hank announced, but his eyes didn't leave the television screen. His arm jerked with disgust when the Raiders fumbled the ball. He mumbled expletive-filled advice to the quarterback. "Ruth didn't sing professionally, but she was a member of the church choir for years. I don't understand about talent. Summer was singing at the top of her lungs from the time she was two. Now Adam, why, he can't carry a tune."

"Me, either." All James could hope was that their children inherited their mother's singing ability.

"Don't worry about it. She loves you anyway."

It took James a moment to realize his father-in-law was completely serious.

"Brunch is ready," Helen announced. "Hank, turn off that blasted football game."

"But, Helen, the score's tied."

"Hank!"

"All right, all right." Reluctantly Hank reached for the TV controller and muted the television. His wife didn't seem to notice, and Hank shared a conspiratorial wink with James. "Compromise," he whispered. "She won't even know."

James sat next to Summer at the table. "This looks delicious," he said to Helen. It was apparent his mother-in-law had gone to a good deal of trouble for this brunch. There was sausage and ham slices and fried strips of bacon, along with what looked to be an egg casserole, fresh-baked sweet rolls and three different kinds of juice.

James noted that Helen waited until everyone had filled their plate until she mentioned the April wedding date. "The reason I wanted to talk to the two of you is about the wedding date." She paused as if she wasn't sure how to proceed. "Being Adam's our son, I didn't have a whole lot to do with the wedding plans when he married Denise. I had no idea we'd need to book the reception hall so far in advance."

"What do you mean?" Summer asked. "I thought you already had the place for the reception."

"It fell through, sweetheart," Hank answered. "Trust me, your mother's done her best. I can't tell you the number of phone calls she's made."

"If we're going to have a nice big wedding the way you deserve," her mother said pointedly, "it'll need to be later than April. My goodness, it takes three to four weeks just to get the invitations printed, and we can't order them until we have someplace *nice* for the reception."

"How much later?" was James's question.

Helen and Hank exchanged looks. "June might work, but September would be best."

"September," Summer cried.

"September's out of the question." With the primary in September, James couldn't manage time away for a wedding. "If we're going to need to wait that long anyway, then let's make it for after the election in November." The minute he made the suggestion, James realized he'd said the wrong thing.

"November." Summer's voice sagged with defeat. "Exactly what am I supposed to do between April and November?"

"Move up to Seattle with James, of course," Hank said without a qualm.

"Absolutely not," Helen protested. "We can't have our daughter living with James before they're married."

"Helen, for the love of heaven, they're already married, remember?"

"Yes, but no one knows that."

"James?"

It seemed everyone turned to him. "Other than my dad, no one knows I'm married, either."

Summer seemed to wilt. "In essence, what you're saying is that you don't want me with you."

"No." James could hear the hurt and disappointment in her voice and wished he knew some magical way to solve the problem, but he didn't. "You know that isn't true."

His wife brushed the hair out of her face. "Why is everything so complicated all at once? It seemed so simple when James and I first decided to do things this way. Now I feel as if we're trapped."

James felt the same way himself. "We'll talk about it and get back to you," he told his in-laws. Both were content to leave it there.

After brunch James and Summer took a walk around her old neighborhood. She didn't say anything for a couple of blocks. Their pace was leisurely. Summer clasped her hands behind her back as if she didn't want to be close to him just then. He gave her the space she needed, but longed to place his arm around her.

"I know you're disappointed, sweetheart, so am I." He felt if he could get her talking about it then they could reason all this out.

"I feel like excess baggage in your life."

"You're never that. You are my life."

"Oh, James, how did everything get so messed up?"

"It's my fault," he muttered, and rammed his fingers through his hair. "I was the one who suggested we go ahead with the wedding right away."

"Thank heaven. I'd hate to think how long we'd need to wait if you hadn't."

"I was being purely selfish and only a little practical. I knew I wasn't going to be able to keep from making love to you much longer."

"And you're gentleman enough to prefer to marry me first," she suggested softly.

"Something like that." She made him sound far more noble than necessary. It could be that it was getting embarrassing to follow her around with his tongue hanging out of the side of his mouth. Marrying her was what he wanted. He wouldn't have suggested it if it hadn't already been on his mind.

"The problem is the election. I had no business marrying you when I did. Not when I knew damn good and well what this year would be like."

"The campaign?"

He nodded. "I've never been a political person."

"I thought judges were nonpartisan."

"They are, but trust me, sweetheart, there's plenty of politics involved. I want this, Summer, but not enough to put you through this."

She was silent again for a long moment. "One question."

"Anything."

She lowered her head and increased her pace as if she needed time to sort through her thoughts. "Why didn't you tell anyone we'd married?"

It was fair enough. "I told my campaign manager that you and I were engaged." James hesitated, carefully selecting his words.

"And?"

"And he asked me to wait until after the election to go through with the wedding. He had a number of reasons, some valid, others not, but he did say one thing that made sense."

"What was that?"

"He reminded me that I was paying him good money to take his advice."

"I see." She gave a short laugh that revealed little if any amusement. "I don't even know who your campaign manager is and already I dislike him."

"Ralph. Ralph Southworth. He isn't so bad."

"What will we do, James?"

"I don't know."

"Do you want to wait until after the election for me to move to Seattle?"

"No," he said vehemently.

"But you can't stop thinking about Ralph's concerns."

"Something like that." They walked past a school yard with a battered chain-link fence. It looked as if every third-grade class for the past twenty years had made it their personal goal to climb that fence.

"I've given this a lot of thought," James told her. It had weighed down his heart for nearly two weeks, ever since his talk with Ralph. "There are no easy solutions."

"We don't need to decide anything right this minute, do we?"

"No." Actually James was relieved. At the moment he was more than willing to say the hell with it and move Summer to Seattle with him.

"Then let's both give it some thought in the next few weeks."

"That sounds like a good idea." He placed his arm around her shoulders. "I've worked a lot of years for this opportunity to sit on the bench, Summer, but it's not worth losing you."

"Losing me?" She laughed and smiled up at him. "You'd have one hell of a time getting rid of me, James Wilkens, and don't you forget it."

James chuckled and lightly kissed her. It was difficult to leave it at that, especially knowing that within a matter of hours he'd be leaving her again. Only this time he didn't know how long it would be before he could be with her again.

Summer rubbed her face against the side of his. "I can remember a time when I had to ask you to kiss me in public."

"That was before you had me completely twisted around your finger." The changes she'd already wrought in his life boggled his mind. "I don't know what I did to deserve you, but whatever it was I'm grateful."

She wrapped her arm around his. "Your flight leaves in less than five hours."

"I know."

"I suppose we should head back to the apartment." She looked up at him and jiggled her delicately shaped eyebrows. "That's plenty of time for what I have in mind."

"Summer..."

"Yes, dear." She batted her eyelashes at him, and James swore he'd never met a woman with longer lashes. They were as seductive as anything he'd ever seen.

They made their farewells to her family and were soon on their way back to her apartment. There was time to make love, he decided, shower and pack, and then he'd be gone again.

She must have been thinking the same thing because Summer said, "It always seems you're leaving me."

James couldn't even tell her it wouldn't be for long. They parked in the lot outside her apartment and as soon as they were out of the car James knew something wasn't right. Summer tensed, her gaze on the man climbing out of the car next to theirs.

"Summer?" James asked.

"It's Jason," she said in a low tone.

"Jason?" It took James far longer than it should have to make the connection. "*The* Jason?"

Her nod was almost imperceptible.

"What's he want?"

"I don't know."

Apparently they were about to find out. He was big—football-player sized—and tanned. Either he was a beachboy or he frequented a tanning booth. He wore faded cutoff jeans, a tank top and several gold chains around his neck.

"Hello, Jason," Summer said stiffly.

"Summer." Now it was the other man's turn to look over at James. "Who's this? A friend of your father's?"

"This is my husband. Kindly leave. We don't have anything to say to each other."

"Your husband?" Jason laughed outright, mocking them both. "You don't honestly expect me to believe that, do you?"

"It's true," James answered. "Now it really would be best if you left like the lady asked."

Jason planted his muscular hands on his lean hips. "You and what army are going to make me walk away from Summer?"

"As I recall, you already left her," James said smoothly, placing himself between Summer and the other man. "I also remember hearing something about you marrying shortly afterward. And didn't I hear, just recently, that you and your wife are expecting a child?"

"We're separated."

"I'm sorry to hear that. Unfortunately Summer and I are now married and she's not interested in starting something with you."

"I don't believe that."

"Oh, honestly, Jason," Summer said with a sorry lack of patience. "Are you such an egotist to believe I'd ever want you back?"

"You love me."

"Loved," she said pointedly. "Past tense."

"Don't give me any bull about you and granddaddy here."

"Granddaddy?" she snapped. "James is ten times the man you'll ever be." She pushed her way past James and glared at her former fiancé. "You know what? Every day of my life I thank God you broke off our engagement—otherwise I'd never have met James. He's taught me what loving someone really means. Which is clearly something you don't have a clue about."

James had Summer by the shoulders. "Honey, it doesn't do any good to argue with him." He looked to Jason, who was red faced and angry. "I think it would be best if you left."

"Stay out of this," Jason snapped.

"We're married and in love," James told him, trying to add reason to a discussion that was fast getting out of hand. "Nothing you have to say is going to change that."

Jason spit on the ground. "She's nothing but a whore anyway."

James would have walked away for almost anything. But he refused to allow anyone to speak derogatorily about Summer. He stepped toward Summer's former fiancé until they were face-to-face. "I suggest you apologize to the lady."

"Gonna make me?"

"Yes," James said tightly. He'd been a schoolboy the last time he was in a fistfight, but he wasn't going to allow this jaded, ugly man to insult Summer.

The two walked a circle around each other.

Jason's hands went up first. He swung at James, who was quick enough to get out of the way of the wildly flung fist. The second time James wasn't so fortunate. The punch hit him squarely in the eye, but James didn't pay attention to the pain since he was more intent on delivering his own.

"James!" Summer repeatedly screamed his name. James could vaguely hear her in the background, pleading with him to stop, that Jason wasn't worth the trouble.

The two men wrestled to the ground, and James was able to level a couple of punches of his own. "You'll apologize," he demanded between gritted teeth when Summer's former fiancé showed signs of wanting to quit.

Blood drooled out of the corner of Jason's mouth, and one eye was swollen. Jason nodded. "Sorry," he muttered.

James released him just in time for the police to arrive.

Chapter Eight

Summer wouldn't have believed James was capable of such anger or violence. Part of her wanted to call him a fool, but another part wanted to tell him how grateful she was for his love and his protection.

His left eye was badly swollen even with the bag of ice she'd given him. James had refused to hold it to his face while he talked to the police.

His black eye wasn't the only damage. His mouth was cut, and an ugly bruise was beginning to form along the underside of his jaw. Jason was in much worse shape, with what looked to be a broken nose.

After talking to both Jason and James and a couple of witnesses, the police asked James if he wanted to press charges. James eyed Jason.

"I don't think that will be necessary. I sincerely doubt that this young man will trouble my wife again. Isn't that right?" he asked, turning to Jason.

Jason wiped the blood from the side of his mouth. "I didn't come here looking for trouble."

"That looks like what you got," the police officer told him. "I'd count my blessings and stay away."

"I'm out of here," Jason said with disgust. He climbed inside his car and slammed the door, then drove off as if he couldn't get away fast enough.

"He won't be back," Summer said confidently. She knew Jason well enough to realize he'd learned his lesson. His ego was too fragile to return after being humiliated.

"You're right, he won't," James insisted darkly, "because you're filing a restraining order against him first thing tomorrow morning."

Summer nodded, wishing she'd thought to do so earlier, but she'd had no idea Jason would do anything like this.

"This isn't the first time he's pestered you, is it?"

Summer lowered her gaze.

"He was the reason you had your phone number changed, isn't it?"

She gave a small, imperceptible nod.

"Why didn't you tell me?"

"What good could you have done from Seattle?"

"You should have told me."

The anger hadn't completely worked its way through James, she feared, and she was about to receive the lecture of her life. When nothing more came, she raised her eyes to her husband and wanted to weep.

His face was a mess. His eye was terribly swollen now. It might have been better if she could have convinced him to apply the ice pack. Anyone looking at him would instantly know he'd been involved in an altercation—her husband the judge, and all because of her.

The police left soon afterward. Summer led the way into her apartment.

"Can I get you anything?" she asked, feeling dreadful about the whole sorry mishap.

"I'm fine."

He wasn't fine, and Summer knew it. His hands were swollen, his knuckles scraped and bleeding. All at once his fingers started to blur, and the room spun. It felt as if everything were closing in on her. Panic-stricken, Summer groped for the kitchen counter and held on until the waves of dizziness passed.

"Honey? What's wrong?"

"Nothing. I got a little light-headed is all." She didn't mention how close she'd come to passing out. Even now she felt the force of her will was the only thing keeping her conscious.

James came to her and placed his arm around her waist and gently guided her into the living room. They sat together on the sofa, and Summer rested her head against his shoulder, wondering what was wrong with her physically for her to feel so crummy all at once.

"I'm so sorry," she whispered, fighting back tears.

"For what?"

"The fight."

"That wasn't your doing."

"But, James, you have a terrible black eye. What will people say?" She hated to think about the speculation he'd face when he returned to Seattle, and it was all on account of her. Perhaps she should have told James that Jason was pestering her, but she hated to burden him with her troubles.

"Everyone will think I was in one hell of a fist-fight," James teased. "It'll probably be the best thing to happen to my reputation in years. People will see me in an entirely new light."

"Everyone will wonder."

"Of course they will, and I'll tell them they should see the other guy."

Summer made an honest effort to laugh but found she couldn't. She twisted her head a bit so she could look at him. The bruise on his jaw was purple and ugly. She raised tentative fingers to it and bit her lower lip when he winced.

"Oh, James." Gently she pressed her lips to the underside of his jaw.

"That helps." He encouraged her.

She kissed him again, easing her mouth toward his. He made several small moans. Before long they were sharing deep, hungry kisses.

"I refuse," James said, unbuttoning her blouse and having difficulty with his swollen hands, "to allow Jason to ruin our last few hours together."

"Me, too." She repositioned herself atop him, straddling his hips. When his fumbling fingers returned to her blouse, she brushed his hands aside and completed the task for him. All the while their lips continued to work against each other in long, deep, needy kisses.

"Does this hurt?" she asked, spreading a series of soft pecks over his face.

"Like crazy."

"Oh." Summer backed away.

"Don't stop," he pleaded. "We're just getting to the interesting part."

She smiled softly and looped her arms around his shoulders. "We have time for a shower," she breathed.

"Yes, but do you have a large enough hot-water tank?"

Summer giggled, recalling their last experience in her compact shower stall and how the water had gone cold at precisely the wrong moment.

The sound of the key turning in the lock alerted Summer to the fact her roommate was back. She sat back abruptly and closed her blouse.

Julie stepped into the living room and tossed her suitcase onto the floor, then hesitated. "I'm not interrupting anything, am I?" Her gaze narrowed. "James? What the hell happened to you?"

James didn't expect his black eye to go unnoticed, but he wasn't prepared for the amount of open curiosity it aroused, either.

"Morning, Judge Wilkens." Betty Jamison, the secretary he shared with two other judges, greeted him by rote when he entered the office bright and early Monday morning. Betty dropped her pencil and pad. "Judge Wilkens," she breathed. "My goodness, what happened?"

He mumbled something about meeting with the wrong end of a fist and hurried into his office. It was clear he was going to need to come up with an explanation that would satisfy the curious.

Brad Williams knocked on his door no less than five minutes later. His fellow judge let himself into James's office and stared. "So it's true?"

"What's true?"

"You tell me. Looks like you've been in one hell of a fight."

"It was a minor scuffle, and that's all I'm going to say about it." James stood and reached for his robe, eager to escape a series of prying questions he didn't want to answer. He had the distinct feeling the rest of the day was going to be like this, as well.

And he was right.

By the time James pulled out of the parking garage that evening, he regretted that he hadn't called in sick. He might have done it if a black eye would disappear in a couple of days, but that wasn't likely to happen. James checked his reflection in the rearview mirror. The eye looked worse than it had the previous day. Puffier, too. He pressed his index finger against the swelling and was surprised by the amount of pain it caused him. The discomfort he didn't mind; it was the unsightliness of the bruises and the questions and curious looks he could live without.

Irritated and not knowing exactly whom to blame, James drove to his father's house. He hadn't been to see Walter in a couple of weeks and was anxious to talk.

His father was working a *New York Times* crossword puzzle when James let himself into the house. He looked up from the folded newspaper and did a double take. To his credit, Walter didn't mention the black eye. "Hello, James."

"Dad."

James walked over to the snifter of Scotch Walter kept on hand and poured himself a liberal amount. He wasn't fond of hard liquor and rarely indulged, but he felt he needed something potent. And fast.

"It's been one of those days, has it?"

James's back was to his father. "You might say that." He took his first sip and bared his teeth as the liquid burned its way down his throat. "This stuff could rot out a man's stomach."

"So I've heard."

Taking the glass with him, James sat in the leather wing-tip chair next to his father. "I suppose you're wondering about the eye."

"I'll admit to being curious."

"You and everyone else I've seen today."

"I can imagine you've been the object of more than one inquisitive stare."

"I was in a fistfight."

"You?"

"Don't sound so surprised. You were the one who told me there would be times in a man's life when he couldn't walk away from a fight. This happened to be one of those unfortunate set of circumstances."

"Do you want to talk about it?" His father relaxed and set aside the newspaper.

"Not particularly, but if you must know, it was over Summer."

"Ah, yes, Summer. How is she? I don't suppose you've managed to get that girl pregnant yet, have you? I'm telling you, son, I like her. Couldn't have chosen a better mate for you had I gone looking myself."

James smiled for the first time that day. "She's fine. I was with her this weekend." James raised the Scotch to his lips and grimaced at the strong taste. "We had brunch with her parents."

"Helen and Hank. Good people," Walter commented.

"There seems to be a problem with the April wedding date. Helen suggested we wait until June."

"Do you want that?" Walter asked.

"No. Neither does Summer."

"Then the hell with it, let her finish out her contract with whomever it was she's singing for and join you then. You've already had a wedding. I never could understand why you wanted two ceremonies. It seemed preposterous to me, but then I'm an old man with little appreciation for fancy weddings. What I would appreciate is a couple of grandkids. I'm not getting any younger, you know, and neither are you."

"Do away with the second ceremony?"

"That's what I said," Walter muttered.

James closed his eyes with relief. Of course. It made perfect sense to him. He'd suggested a second ceremony because he thought that was what Summer wanted, but James suspected that if he asked her, he'd learn otherwise.

"How'd you get so smart?" James asked his father.

"Don't know, but I must be very wise," Walter said, and chuckled. "I've got a superior court judge for a son."

James laughed and it felt good.

"Stay for dinner," the elder Wilkens insisted. "It's been a while since the two of us spent any real time together. Afterward you can let me beat you in a game of chess, and I'll go to bed a happy man."

"All right." It was an invitation too good to refuse.

By the time James made it to his house, it was past eight. The light on his answering machine was blinking as if it were all the machine could do not to shout out its long list of messages. Frankly James was tempted to ignore the machine.

He jerked his tie back and forth several times in an effort to loosen it. He was tired but mellow and not particularly interested in returning a long list of phone calls. Especially when he suspected most were curious to learn what they could about his mysterious black eye.

The only person he wanted to talk to was Summer. He ignored the answering machine and reached for the phone. She answered on the second ring.

"I just got in," he explained. "Dad and I had dinner."

"Did you give him my love?"

"I did better than that—I let him beat me in chess."

She laughed, and James closed his eyes and savored the melodic sound of her laughter. It was like a balm after the uncomfortable day he'd endured.

"How's the eye?"

"Good." So he lied. "Say, shouldn't you be on stage about now?"

"Yeah, but I seem to have come down with the flu. I've felt crummy all day. When I woke up this morning, I was terribly sick. At first I thought it was nerves over what happened with Jason, but it didn't go away, so I had to call in sick."

"Have you been to a doctor?"

"No. Have you?"

She had him there. "No."

"I'll be fine. I just want to be sure I didn't give you the flu bug while you were here."

"I'm fine."

They must have talked for fifteen minutes more, saying nothing yet sharing the most important details of their lives. Their conversation would have gone on a good while longer, James suspected, had someone not rung his doorbell.

It was Ralph Southworth. His campaign manager took one look at James and dramatically threw his arms in the air. "What the hell happened to you?"

"A good evening to you, too," James said evenly.

Ralph rammed all ten fingers through his hair with enough force for it to hurt. "Don't you listen to your answering machine? I've left no less than five messages, and you haven't bothered to return one."

"Sit down." James advised calmly. "Do you want something to drink?"

Ralph's gaze narrowed as he studied James's face. "Am I going to need it?"

"That depends." James pointed to the recliner by the large brick fireplace. He would tell Ralph the truth because it was necessary and, knowing his campaign manager's feelings for Summer, he suspected Ralph would need a stiff drink. "Make yourself at home."

Instead, Ralph insisted on following him into the kitchen. "I got no less than ten phone calls this afternoon asking about your black eye. You can't show up and say little or nothing."

"I can't?" This was news to James, since he'd done exactly that all day. "I thought you were here to discuss business."

"I am." Ralph frowned when James brought the hard liquor out of a top cabinet. "So you suspect I'm going to need that."

"Yes." James didn't believe in holding back.

"I met with the League of Women Voters and have arranged for you to speak at their luncheon in July. It's a real coup, James, and I hope you appreciate my efforts."

Frankly this was what he was paying Ralph to do for him, but in light of his recent troubles, now didn't seem the proper time to mention it.

"Now tell me about the eye."

"All right," James said, and added two ice cubes to the glass, filled it a third full with bourbon and handed it to his friend. "I got hit in the face with a fist."

"Whose fist?"

"A beach bum by the name of Jason. I don't remember his last name, if I ever heard it."

Ralph swallowed his first sip of liquor. "Does the beachboy have anything to do with the woman you mentioned not long ago?"

"Yeah."

The two men stared across the kitchen from each other in a silent battle of wills.

"Were the police called?" Ralph demanded.

It took James a moment to own up to the truth. "Yes."

Ralph slammed his hand against the counter. "I should have known. Damn it all to hell, James, what did I tell you? A woman is nothing but trouble. Mark my words, if you get involved any further with Spring..."

"Summer."

"Whatever her name is doesn't matter, because she spells just one thing. Trouble. You've worked your entire career as an attorney for this opportunity. This is your one shot at the bench, James. We both know it. You asked me to manage your campaign and I agreed, but I thought it would be a team effort. The two of us.''

"It is.'' James wanted to hold on to his seat on the bench more than he'd wanted anything, other than to marry Summer. It was the key to a long list of career goals. He also felt that he was the best man for the position. To be this close and lose it all now would be bittersweet indeed.

"Then why,'' Ralph asked, his palms exposed, "are you sabotaging your own campaign?''

"I'm not doing it on purpose.''

"Stay away from this woman.''

"Ralph, I can't. I won't.''

Ralph rubbed a hand down his face. It was clear he was frustrated and growing more so by the minute.

"Summer's in California, but I plan on bringing her to Seattle as soon as it can be arranged.''

"Tell me you're joking.''

"I'm not.'' As far as James could see, he'd best admit to the truth now and be done with it. "We're married.''

Ralph reached for a chair and sank into it. "When?''

"Over New Year's.''

"What?'' Ralph said this as if he didn't believe him.

"It was just one of those things. We fell in love and were married. We were hoping for a more elaborate ceremony later, but that's going to be a problem.''

"If you want to know what's a problem, James, it's the marriage. Why didn't you tell me about it right away?''

"I should have,'' James admitted, sorry now that he hadn't. "But when you said you'd never been in love,

I didn't think there was much of a chance you'd understand what we'd done."

"What you've done, James, is jeopardize your entire campaign."

Somehow he sincerely doubted that. "It seems to me you're overreacting."

"Time will tell, won't it?" Ralph asked smugly.

James decided to ignore that. "If anything, Summer will be an asset. Unfortunately her contract doesn't expire with Disney until April."

"That's right," Ralph said sarcastically. "I forgot, she's a show girl."

"A singer and an actress and a very talented one at that," James boasted.

"An actress, a show girl, they're both the same."

"When she's finished with her contract, I want her to move in with me."

"Here in Seattle?" To hear Ralph, he made it sound like a world-class disaster.

"A wife belongs with her husband."

"What about the beachboy?"

James frowned. "We don't need to worry about him. He's gone for good."

"I certainly hope so. And while we're making out a wish list, let's add a couple of other facts to it. Let's wish that your worthy opponent doesn't find out about this little skirmish between you and Summer's previous lover boy. Let's make a great big wish that he doesn't discover that the police were called and a report filed."

"He won't," James said confidently, far more confidently than what he was feeling.

"I certainly hope you're right," Ralph said, and downed what was left of the glass of bourbon in one last gulp. He hit the glass against the counter when he finished. "Now tell me, what damage did you do to the beachboy?"

"You didn't tell him, did you?" Julie said when Summer set the telephone receiver back in its proper place.

"No," she admitted reluctantly. She placed her hand protectively against her stomach.

"A man has a right to know he's going to be a father," Julie said, bit into an apple and sank, tucking her feet beneath her, onto the sofa.

Summer closed her eyes. Even hearing food made her sick to her stomach. In the past two months she'd seen parts of toilets that weren't meant to be examined at such close range. She hadn't kept down a single breakfast in two weeks. The day before she wondered why she even bothered to eat it. Dumping it directly into the toilet would save time and trouble.

"Just how long do you think James is going to fall for you having the flu?"

It had been over a month since she'd last seen James, and in that time Summer had lost ten pounds. Her clothes hung on her, and she was as pale as death. Summer felt as if she spent more time at the doctor's office than she did at her own apartment. Her biggest fear was that with her being so desperately ill most of the time, there was something wrong with the baby.

"Why haven't you told him?" Julie wanted to know.

"It just doesn't seem to be the thing to do over the phone." Besides, she remembered James mentioning that a pregnancy now would be a disaster. Well, she hadn't gotten this way by herself!

She knew exactly when it had happened, too. There could only be the one time when they hadn't used protection. James was the one who'd insisted that it would be all right that once. Well, he was wrong.

"When are you going to see him again?"

Summer brushed the hair away from her face. "I don't know."

"You talk every night on the phone. He sends you gifts. I don't know anyone else who got six dozen red roses for Valentine's Day."

"He tends to be extravagant when it comes to me."

"Extravagant with everything but his time."

"He's so busy, Julie. I never realized how much there was to being a superior court judge, and he really cares about the people he works with. Not just those who stand before him to be sentenced, either, but the attorneys and his staff, too. Then there's the election."

"Then go to him. He's just as unhappy without you."

"I've only got three weeks left on my contract, and..."

"Do you honestly think no one's figured out you're pregnant? Think about it, Summer. You came back from Vegas all happy and in love, and two weeks later you're routinely heaving your guts out after every meal. No one's asking you to perform when you feel this crummy."

"But..."

"Do everyone a favor and—" Julie stopped when the doorbell chimed. "Are you expecting anyone?"

"No." Summer laid her head back against the sofa and drew in several deep breaths, hoping that would ease the bout of nausea.

"It's for you," Julie said, looking over her shoulder. "He claims his name is Walter Wilkens, and even without the black eyes, I'd say James bears a strong resemblance to him."

Summer threw aside the blanket and scurried off the sofa, anxious to see her father-in-law. "Walter?" What could he possibly be doing here? "Come inside, please."

The refined, older gentleman stepped into the apartment and removed his hat. "Summer?" His gaze narrowed when he looked at her. "James said you'd been ill with the flu, but my dear..."

"She looks dreadful," Julie finished for him. Her roommate took another noisy bite of her apple. "I'm Julie, by the way, Summer's roommate and best friend."

"Sit down, please," Summer said, motioning toward the only chair in the house without blankets or clean laundry stacked on it.

"Would you like something to drink?" Julie asked.

"No...no, thank you." It seemed the cat had stolen her father-in-law's tongue. "Summer, my dear." He frowned. "Have you been to a doctor?"

"Several times," Julie answered, chewing on her apple. "Three times this week, right, Summer?"

"Julie," she snapped.

"Are you going to tell him or not?"

Summer tossed the tangled curls over her shoulder and groaned inwardly. "I don't have much choice now, do I?" She met James's father's eyes and discovered her lower lip was trembling. She bit into it, certain she was about to do something silly like burst into tears. Her emotions were on a teeter-totter, along with everything else in her body that had suddenly gone wacko.

"Summer, what is it?" Walter prodded.

"I'm pregnant," she whispered, and smiled happily while tears streamed down her ashen cheeks.

Walter bolted out of his chair. "Hot damn!"

"Other than me, you're the first person she's told," Julie felt obliged to tell him. "Not even her own family knows, although her mother would take one look at her and guess."

"James doesn't know?"

"Nope." Again it was Julie who supplied the answer.

"And why not?"

"A woman doesn't tell a man that sort of thing over the phone," Summer insisted. She needed to see his face, to gauge James's reaction so she'd know what he was really thinking when he learned the truth.

"She's been sicker than a dog."

"Thank you, Julie, but I can take it from here."

"I can see that," Walter said, ignoring Summer.

"What brings you to California?" Summer asked cordially, looking for a way of changing the subject.

"A business trip. I thought James might have mentioned it."

If he had, Summer had missed hearing it. She had the feeling she'd been doing a lot of that lately.

"Well, my dear," Walter said, sitting back in the chair and grinning so broadly he exposed a mouthful of perfect white teeth. "This is a pleasant surprise."

"It was one for me, too."

"I can just see James's face when you tell him."

"He probably won't know what to do, laugh or cry."

"He'll probably do a little of both."

For his part, Walter was laughing, Summer noticed. He hadn't stopped smiling from the moment he heard the news.

"Everything has always been carefully planned in James's life," Walter said, grinning cheekily. "Then he met you. Bingo, he's a husband, and now it seems he's about to be a father. This is terrific news, just terrific news."

"James might not find it all that wonderful," Summer said, voicing her fears for the first time. "He's in the middle of an important campaign."

"Phooey. Don't you worry about a thing."

"I am worried."

"Then we're going to have to do something about that."

"We are?" Summer asked.

"Of course we are. It seems to me that if my son's about to be a father, that you should tell him, and the sooner the better. Pack your things, Summer. It's about time you moved to Seattle where you belong. You need your husband."

"But..."

"Don't argue with me, young lady. I'm an old man and I'm accustomed to having my own way. You're worried, and we're going to put an end to speculation here and now."

Chapter Nine

Something was wrong with Summer. James had sensed it for weeks. He would have confronted her and demanded answers if she didn't sound so fragile.

There was that business with the flu, but just exactly how long was the malady going to last? When he asked her what the doctors said, she seemed vague and uneasy.

Part of the problem, James realized, was the length of time they'd spent apart. He hadn't meant for it to be so long between visits. Summer had intended to come to Seattle, but that had fallen through just as his last visit to California had. Neither of them was happy about it, but frankly there was nothing James could have done on his end. He was certain that was the case with her, too.

James sat at his desk in the den and fretted. Sometimes when he needed to mull over a problem, he would pace. Lately he'd damn near worn a pathway in the thick carpet. He couldn't sit still and not agonize over the situation with Summer. He felt helpless and frustrated. Despite Ralph's dire warnings, he wished he'd brought Summer back to Seattle to live with him. This separation was hurting them both.

Worries hounded him like dogs nipping at his heels. His greatest fear was that Summer regretted their marriage. He, after all, had been the one who'd suggested they go ahead with the ceremony then and there.

Their telephone conversations weren't the same. He felt as if Summer were hiding something from him. It used to be that any subject was safe, but he noticed how she steered him away from certain topics. She didn't want to talk about herself or her job or this flu bug that had kept her down for the past few weeks. It used to be they could speak for hours; now he had the feeling she was eager to get off the line.

James wondered about Jason, but when he asked, Summer assured him she hadn't seen him since the fight.

The fight.

His black eye had caused a great deal of speculation among his peers. James had made no explanation. By way of the grapevine, he heard Ralph's version and found it only distantly related to the truth. According to his campaign manager, James had been jumped by gang members and valiantly fought them off until the police arrived.

When James confronted Ralph with the story, the other man smiled and said he couldn't be held accountable for rumors. Right or wrong, James had let the matter drop. He was eager to put the incident behind him.

James certainly hadn't expected married life to be this lonely. He'd never felt this lonesome, this detached from the mainstream of everyday life, or this isolated. Missing Summer was like having acid eat at his stomach. Only a store-bought tablet wasn't going to cure what ailed him.

His desk was filled with demands. Demands on his time. Demands on his emotions. He was weary. Unsure of his marriage. Lost and impatient.

He went into the kitchen to microwave himself a cup of instant coffee when he saw a car turn into his driveway and curve around to the backyard.

His father.

Frankly James wondered why his father would stop by unannounced on a Sunday afternoon. He wasn't in the mood for company, but then again maybe a sounding board might be exactly what he needed. Other than his father, there was no one with whom he could discuss the situation with Summer.

The slam of one car door closing was followed almost immediately by another. James frowned. Dad had brought someone with him. Great. Just great.

James took the hot water out of the microwave, added the coffee granules and stirred briskly. The knock against the back door came next.

"Come in, the door's open," he called, not turning around. He didn't feel like being necessarily polite. Not this day, when it felt as if the world was closing in around him.

He sipped his coffee and stared out the window. The daffodils were blooming, and the—

"Hello, James."

James whirled around. "Summer?" He couldn't believe she was real. It was impossible. A figment of his imagination. An apparition. Before another second passed, James walked across the kitchen and swept her into his arms.

Laughing and sobbing both at once, Summer hugged him close, and James realized he was having trouble with his heart. It refused to beat. It was as if everything were so beautiful and perfect in that millisecond he needed to hold on to it for an extra space in time.

They were kissing each other. She him. He her. Neither could give or get enough.

Walter stood in the background and cleared his throat. "I'll wait for the two of you in the living room," he said loud enough to be sure he was heard.

As far as James was concerned, his father should make himself comfortable. This could take a while. He had a lot of lost time to make up for, and the way he felt just then, it wouldn't be over any time soon.

Summer in his arms was the closest thing to heaven James had ever found. Only then did he notice how thin and frail she was. The flu bug had ravaged her body.

"Sweetheart," he whispered between kisses. He paused and brushed the hair away from her face in order to get a good look at her.

She was terribly pale. Her once pink cheeks were colorless, and her eyes appeared sunken and rimmed with dark circles. "Are you over the flu?"

She lowered her gaze and stepped away from him. "I . . . you'd better sit down, James."

"Sit down. But why?"

Her hands closed around the back of a kitchen chair. "I have something important to tell you."

He could see that she was nervous and on the verge of tears. The worries that were nipping at his heels earlier returned with reinforcements. Summer had more than a common flu bug.

"Just tell me," he said stiffly. A knot was beginning to form in his stomach at the long list of possibilities. Was it cancer or something equally life threatening? The knot twisted and tightened.

"I don't have the flu," she whispered.

James could see that she'd been terribly ill. Whatever it was must be very bad for his father to bring her to Seattle.

"How serious is it?" he asked, unwilling to beat around the bush. He preferred to confront whatever they were dealing with head-on.

"It's serious, James, very serious." Slowly she raised her eyes to his. "We're going to have a baby."

His relief was so great that he nearly laughed. "A baby? You mean to tell me you're pregnant?"

"That's what it generally means." Her fingers had gone white, and she was watching him closely.

James took her in his arms. "I thought you were really sick."

"I have been really sick," she told him crisply. "Morning sickness. Afternoon sickness. Evening sickness. I...I can't seem to keep food down... I've never been more miserable in my life."

"My feeling is that part of her problem has been psychological," Walter announced from where he was standing in the doorway. "The poor girl's been worried sick about how you were going to take the news."

"Me?"

"My feelings exactly," Walter said. "The deed's done, what's there to think about? It seems to me that the two of you have far greater concerns than the small matter of an unexpected pregnancy. Besides you've made me an extremely happy man."

"A baby." James remained awestruck with the news.

"Now tell him your due date, Summer—he'll get a real kick out of that."

"September seventh," Summer announced.

Everyone seemed to be studying him, looking for a reaction. Hell, James didn't know what to think. Then it hit him. "September seventh? That's the date of the primary."

"I know. Isn't it a kick?" Walter asked.

"How long can you stay?" James asked, taking Summer's hands in his own. His head was buzzing.

Summer looked to Walter.

"Stay," his father barked. "My dear son, this is your wife. I brought her to Seattle so she can live with you. This is where she belongs."

"You can live with me?" A man could only take so much news in at one time. Good or bad. First off he learned his wife didn't have a life-threatening disease. Then he discovered he was going to be a father, but more importantly he was going to have the opportunity to prove exactly what kind of husband he yearned to be.

James pulled out the chair and sat Summer in it. Then he knelt on the floor in front of her and captured her hands in his. "A baby."

"You're sure you don't mind?"

"Of course he doesn't mind," Walter insisted, "and if he does I'll set up an appointment with a good psychiatrist I know. This is the best news we've had in thirty years."

"When did it happen?" James asked.

Summer laughed at him. "You mean to tell me you don't remember?" She leaned toward him and whispered, reminding him of the one episode the morning after their honeymoon night.

"Ah, yes," James said, and chuckled. "As I recall, I was the one who claimed one time wouldn't matter."

"I don't suppose there's anything to eat in this house?" Walter asked, banging cupboard doors open and closed.

"Why have you been so ill?" James wanted to know. It worried him. "Is it routine?"

"My doctor claims some women suffer with severe morning sickness the first few months. He's been wonderful and reassuring. I try to remember that when I'm losing my most recent meal."

"Is there anything that can help?" He was thinking that in these modern times medical science would have discovered a drug that would ease her discomfort.

"She's got what she needs now," Walter insisted.

Summer laid her head on his shoulder. "I was concerned you'd be upset with me."

"Why would I possibly be angry when the most beautiful woman in the world tells me she's having my baby?" He reached for her hand and pressed her palm over his heart. "Notice anything different?" he asked.

She shook her head.

"My heart feels like it's going to burst wide-open."

"Why?"

"Because I'm so happy. We're going to have a baby, Summer. Your body is nurturing my child, and I feel like I could conquer the world."

He wanted his words to reassure her. The last thing he expected was for her to burst into tears.

"But you said a baby would be a disaster just now," she reminded him.

"I said that?"

"He said that?" Walter fumed, and glared at James.

"I don't remember saying it," James told him. "I'm sorry, my love. Just knowing we're going to have a baby makes me far happier than I have any right to be."

"Damn straight he's happy," Walter tossed in, "or there'd be hell to pay. I should have been a grandfather two or three times over before now. As far as I'm concerned, James owes me."

"I'll try and make up for lost time," James promised his father, and comforted Summer by gently patting her back. Damn but it felt good to have her in his arms. Better than anything he'd felt in a good long while.

Summer couldn't remember ever being so hungry. She'd been with James a week and had settled so contentedly into her new life that it was almost as if she'd always been a part of his life.

"Would you like another piece of apple pie?" James asked. "Better yet, why don't we buy the entire thing and take it home with us?"

"Can we do that?" Summer was certain her appetite was a source of embarrassment to James. They'd come down to the Seattle waterfront, one of Summer's favorite places, to a sidewalk restaurant. Summer couldn't decide between the French onion soup and the Cobb Salad, and so she'd ordered both. Then she'd topped off the meal with a huge slice of apple pie à la mode.

"I'll ask the waitress," James said as if it were perfectly normal to order a whole pie for later.

"Have I embarrassed you?" she asked, keeping her voice low.

The corners of James's mouth quivered. "No, but I will admit I've rarely seen anyone enjoy their food more."

"Oh, James, you have no idea how good it is to be able to eat and keep everything down. I feel a thousand times better in this last week than I have in the whole previous two months."

"Then Dad was right," he said.

"About what?"

"The psychological effects of the pregnancy were taking their toll along with the physical. In other words, you were already miserable and making yourself more so. I could kick myself."

"Why?"

"For not guessing. You have to forgive me, sweetheart, I'm new to this husband business."

"You're forgiven."

"Just promise me one thing. Don't keep any more secrets from me, all right?"

She smiled. "You've got yourself a deal."

"James?" A striking-looking couple approached their table.

"Rich and Jamie Manning." Sounding genuinely pleased, James stood and exchanged handshakes with the man. Then he turned to Summer. "Summer, these are two good friends of mine, Rich and Jamie Manning. This is my wife.''

"Your wife?'' Rich repeated, doing a poor job of disguising his surprise. "When did all this happen?''

"Shortly after the New Year,'' James explained. "Would you care to join us?''

"Unfortunately we can't,'' Rich said, "but this is great news. I hope there's a good reason I didn't get a wedding invitation.''

"A very good one,'' James said, grinning. "I've been meaning to let everyone know. It's one of those matters that slip through the cracks.''

"Well, the word's out now,'' Jamie said, smiling at Summer. "Once Rich's mother hears about this, she's going to want to throw a party in your honor.'' Jamie and her husband shared a private, happy look. Summer could see that the couple was deeply in love.

"I'd better give your parents a call before I alienate them completely,'' James said.

"I'll be seeing you soon,'' Rich said, and patted James's shoulder as he passed by.

James was silent for a moment, and Summer wasn't sure if he was pleased or not that his friends had stopped. She didn't think he intended to keep their marriage a secret. Yet he hadn't made a point of introducing her around, either.

"Is there a problem?'' she asked.

"None. It's just that I was hoping to give you some time to regain your strength before introducing you to my friends. We best think about it soon.''

Summer's gaze followed the couple as they made their way toward the front of the restaurant.

"They're happy, aren't they?''

It took Summer a moment to realize James's gaze had followed her own. "Rich and Jamie?"

"Yes." He relaxed against the back of his chair. "They came to see me a few years back with the most unusual request of my career." He smiled, and Summer guessed he must have been amused at the time, as well.

"What did they want?"

"They asked that I draw up a paper for a marriage of convenience."

"Really." That seemed odd to Summer. Although she'd only just met the couple, it was clear to her that they were deeply in love.

"They'd come up with some harebrained scheme about having a child together. Rich would be the sperm donor."

"Did they have a baby?"

"Yes, but Stephanie was conceived the old-fashioned way without a single visit to a medical laboratory."

Summer shook her head. "This doesn't make the least bit of sense to me. Why would two healthy people go to such lengths to arrange a marriage of convenience in order to produce a child? Especially when they're perfectly capable of doing things...the usual way?"

"It does sound a bit silly, doesn't it?"

"Frankly, yes."

"It seems," James said, leaning forward and placing his elbows on the table, "Jamie and Rich had been friends for years. Since their high school days, if I recall correctly. Jamie couldn't seem to fall in love with the right kind of man and, after a couple of disastrous relationships, she announced she was giving up dating altogether.''

''I love the tricks life plays on people,'' Summer said, licking the last of the melted ice cream off her spoon. She looked across the table at the last dab on James's plate. ''Are you going to eat that?'' she asked.

He pushed the plate toward her.

''Thanks,'' she said, and blew him a kiss. ''Go on,'' she encouraged, scooping up the drippings from his pie and ice cream. ''What happened?''

''Apparently Jamie was completely comfortable with her decision, except for the part about a child. That was when she approached Rich, as her good friend, about being the sperm donor for her child.''

''Just between friends, that sort of thing?''

''Exactly. At any rate, Rich didn't think it was such a bad idea himself, the not-marrying part. He'd had his own ups and downs in the relationship department, but the more he got to thinking about her suggestion, the more problems he had with being nothing more than the sperm donor. He was the one who suggested they be married so their child could have his name. He also wanted a say in the baby's upbringing. As I recall, there were a number of other stipulations.''

''And Jamie agreed to all this?''

''She wanted a child.''

''So they came to have you draw everything up?''

''Yes, but I do have to tell you I had my reservations.''

''I can imagine.'' With his ice cream gone, she licked the back of his spoon.

''As I understand it, they have two children now.''

"Well, this marriage of convenience certainly worked to their advantage," Summer told him.

"It sure did."

While she was looking around the table for anything left to eat, she noticed James's gaze studying her. "How are you feeling?" he asked.

"A thousand times better." She smiled and lowered her voice so he alone could hear. "If what you're really asking is if I'm well enough to make love, the answer is yes."

His Adam's apple jerked up and down his throat.

"Shall we hurry home, James?"

"By all means."

He paid the tab and they were gone. "You're sure?" he asked as he unlocked the car door. He helped her inside.

Sitting in the passenger seat, Summer smiled up at her husband. "Am I sure? James, it's been months since we last made love. I swear I'm so hot for you I could pop."

James literally ran around the front of the car. He sped the entire way home. Summer considered it fortunate that they weren't stopped by a traffic cop. She would have liked to have her husband explain his way out of a speeding ticket.

"Torture ... every night for a week," James mumbled as he pulled into the driveway. "I couldn't trust myself to so much as touch you."

"I know."

Her time in Seattle hadn't started out well. Her first morning, she'd woken and run straight for the bathroom. James helped her off the floor when she'd finished. He'd cradled her in his arms and told her how much he loved her for having his baby.

Her first few dinners hadn't stayed down, either. But each day since her arrival, the nausea and episodes of vomiting had become less and less frequent. One week following her arrival, she was almost her old self again.

"This morning," she whispered seductively.

"Yes?"

"When I was dressing I tried on one of our wedding gifts."

James frowned.

"Remember what Julie gave us?"

His Adam's apple bobbed a second time. "The tassels?"

"Yup."

"You're wearing those now?"

She nodded.

James nearly drove the car straight through the garage. "You can't tell a man something like that when he's driving," he barked.

"And why can't I?"

"Because...for the love of heaven, Summer, do you realize how crazy I've been for you?" He continued to jabber as he climbed out of the car and around to her side to help her out. When he opened the car door, she hooped her arms around her husband's neck and kissed him. It seemed the only way to silence him.

James groaned and swung her into his arms.

"What are you doing?" she asked when he carried her toward the house.

"Carrying you over the threshold," he announced. "You've been cheated out of just about everything else when it comes to this marriage—I refuse to rob you of this."

"I haven't been cheated."

"You should have had the big church wedding with all the trimmings."

"Are we going to argue about that again? Really, James, I'd much rather we just made love."

He had a bit of a problem getting the door unlocked while holding her, but he managed. The minute they were inside, he started kissing her, doing the wonderful, exotic things with his tongue that excited her to the point of desperation.

Summer kicked off her shoes.

James kissed her and unsnapped the button to her skirt. The zipper hissed open. All the while he was silently urging her toward the stairs.

Her jacket went next, followed by her shirt.

She made it to the stairway and held her hand out to her husband. James didn't need to be encouraged. He stripped off her panty hose on the stairway as they raced toward the bedroom.

Summer fell upon the bed laughing. "Oh, James, promise me you'll always love me this much."

"I promise you." He tried to remove his shirt without taking off his tie first, with hilarious results. With her arms around her stomach, Summer doubled over laughing. It was a pure act of kindness that she climbed off the bed and loosened the tie enough to slip it over his head. Otherwise, she feared her normally patient, calm husband would have strangled himself.

"You think this is funny, do you?"

"I think you're the most wonderful man alive. Will you always want me this much?"

"I can't imagine not wanting you."

The bed creaked as she lowered herself back onto the mattress and held her arms open to him.

"I've needed you so much," James whispered.

"I think we're both a little crazy."

James took hold of her hips and, pressing her still, he entered her slowly, gently.

A shudder of pleasure rippled through Summer, and she sighed deeply. Biting into her lower lip, she rolled her head to one side.

Carefully, as if he feared hurting their child, he eased himself deeper inside her. Summer bucked several times beneath him, seeking the red-hot pleasure.

"Summer..."

"I know, I know," she whimpered, "but I can't help it."

"What about the baby?"

"I suggest you take care of the mommy and worry about the baby later," she advised him.

"It won't hurt the baby?"

"This is a fine time to be asking me that. No, James, now kindly make love to me."

He did exactly that with a crazed intensity. Summer wasn't sure when it happened, but at some point in the middle of their lovemaking, the bed broke.

Summer didn't care and she was convinced James didn't even notice.

James was half-asleep when he heard the doorbell chime. He would have ignored it, but on the off chance it was someone important, he decided to check the front and see if he recognized the car.

That was a big mistake.

Ralph Southworth stood at his front door.

James grabbed his pants, kissed Summer on the cheek and hurried down the stairs. He found Summer's panty hose and, with all the force he could muster, threw them up the stairs. They floated onto the banister, dangling from the railing.

James took a second to compose himself before he opened the door. "Hello, Ralph." Standing shoeless, James quickly went about buttoning his shirt.

Ralph frowned. "What the hell have you been doing...never mind, I already know the answer to that. Must you really, James?"

"Summer's here."

"So I see."

"Give her a few minutes, and she'll be down so you can meet her," James told him. He sat down in the chair and put on his shoes and socks. "What can I do for you?"

"A number of things, but mainly I'd..." He hesitated as Summer made her way down the stairs. She had the look of a woman well loved. Her hair was mussed, and her eyes were all soft and loving.

"Ralph, this is my wife Summer," James said proudly, joining her. He slipped his arm around her shoulders.

"Hello, Summer," Ralph said stiffly.

"Hello."

"When did you arrive?"

"Last week. Would you two like some coffee? I'll make a pot. James, take your friend into the den, why don't you, and I'll bring everything in there."

James didn't want his wife waiting on him, but something about the way she spoke told him this wasn't the time to argue. It was then that James's gaze fell on the shiny gold tassels. One was draped across a porcelain floral arrangement displayed on a table, and the other was dangling from the chandelier above the entryway.

The heat circled his ears like water through a pipeline. It demanded every ounce of willpower he possessed not to burst out laughing.

"This way, Ralph," he said, ushering the other man into the den.

He saw Summer delicately scoop up a number of clothing items and hurry into the kitchen.

"Something amuses you?"

James cleared his throat. "Not really."

"First of all, James, I feel I must question your judgment. When you claimed you'd married a show girl—"

"Summer's an actress."

"As I said earlier, I don't see much distinction between one or the other. Now," Ralph said stiffly, "as I was saying, I have some reservations regarding your judgment."

This was a serious accusation, considering James was running for a position on the superior court.

Ralph pinched his lips together. "It worries me considerably that you'd marry an unknown on the spur of the moment."

"Love sometimes happens like that."

"Perhaps," Ralph muttered. "Personally I wouldn't know, but James, really, how much younger is she than you?"

"It's not as much as it looks. Eight years."

"She's entirely unsuitable."

"For whom? You? Listen, Ralph, I asked you to manage my campaign, not run my life. I married Summer, and she's going to have my child."

"The girl's pregnant, as well?"

"These things happen between married people. Yes, the baby's due September seventh."

Ralph's thin lips went white with disapproval. "I wonder if she could have chosen a more inconvenient date."

"I don't think it really matters."

"That's the date of the primary election."

"I'm well aware of that."

"Good grief, James," Ralph said, and rubbed his hand down his face. "This simply won't do. It just won't. Once people learn what you've done, they'll assume you were obligated to marry the girl. The last thing we need now is to have your morals questioned."

"Ralph, you're overreacting. Settle down."

"I can't believe you've brought her here, after everything I said to you."

James gritted his teeth. "She's my wife."

Ralph paced and rammed his fingers through his hair. Finally he turned and stared at James and shook his head. "I don't feel I have any choice," he muttered finally.

"Choice about what?"

"I'm resigning as your manager," he announced.

Summer appeared just then, carrying a tray. "Coffee, anyone?"

Chapter Ten

It amazed Summer how easily she settled into life with James. She adored her husband and treasured each moment that they were together.

Her days quickly followed a routine of sorts. She rose early and, because she was feeling better, resumed her regular workout, which included a two-mile run first thing in the morning.

James insisted upon running with her although he made it clear he didn't enjoy traipsing through dark streets at dawn's early light. But he refused to allow her to run alone. So he joined her, whining and protesting every step of the way.

James was naturally athletic, and Summer didn't think anyone was more surprised than her own husband by how enjoyable he found the exercise routine. After their run, they showered together. Thankfully

James's hot-water tank was larger than the meager one back in her Orange County apartment.

This was both good and bad. The negatives came when James, a stickler for punctuality, was late for court two mornings in a row.

"You shower first," he told her following their Monday morning run.

"Not together?" she asked, disappointed.

"I can't be late this morning."

"We'll be good," she promised.

James snickered. "I can't be good with you, Summer. You tempt me too damn much."

"All right, you shower first, and I'll get us breakfast."

He hesitated before he agreed.

A few minutes later he joined Summer in the kitchen where she was pouring two tall glasses of orange juice. He was dressed in his dark business suit and carried his briefcase with him, ready for his workday.

"What are your plans?" he asked, downing the juice. He carried the bagel and cream cheese to the table and pulled out a chair.

"I'm going to see about having that bed fixed once and for all," she said, sharing a knowing look with her husband. "We've broken it three times in the last week."

"They just don't make furniture the way they used to," James grumbled.

Summer couldn't help it; she started to laugh. "I'm not sure the problem's with the bed."

"Just don't try to fix it yourself, understand?"

"Yes, dear," she replied dutifully. "Then later I thought I'd stop in at the library and volunteer to read during story time."

"Good idea," he replied absently as his gaze scanned the newspaper.

Summer knew that his morning ritual included reading the paper, which was something he didn't have as much time for since her arrival. She drank the last bit of her juice and kissed his cheek.

"I'm going upstairs for my shower," she told him.

"All right. Have a good day."

"I will. Oh, before you go, what time will you be home tonight?" she asked.

"Six or so," he mumbled absently, and turned over the front page.

Summer hesitated. His schedule had changed. Rarely had he arrived home before seven the first week after she moved in with him. Each night, it seemed, there was someone to meet, some campaign supporter to talk to, some plans to outline. All had something to do with the September primary, even though it was still months away.

In the past week James had come directly home from the courthouse. Not that she was complaining, but she couldn't help wondering.

"What about your campaign?" she asked.

"Everything's under control," was all he said.

Summer wondered.

All at once James looked up startled, as if he just remembered something. "What day's your ultrasound scheduled?"

"Thursday next week. Don't look so concerned, you don't need to be there."

"I'm coming," he stated emphatically. "Our baby's first picture. I wouldn't miss it for the world. Besides, I'm curious to know if we're going to be blessed with a son or daughter."

"Don't tell me," she insisted. "I don't want to know."

"I won't," he said, and chuckled. He reached out and flattened his hand over her abdomen. "It astonishes me how much I can love this little tyke, and he isn't even born yet."

"He?" she asked, bracing her hands against her hips in mock offense.

"Or whatever the market bears. A daughter would suit me just fine. Actually Dad's hoping for a granddaughter. It's been a good long while since there's been a little girl in the family."

Summer pressed her hand over her husband's. She'd never been this happy. It frightened her sometimes when she thought about it. Experience had taught her that happiness almost always came with a price.

Walter joined them for dinner Wednesday evening. From the moment she'd met him, Summer had found her father-in-law to be a pure delight.

"Did you know Summer could cook this well when you married her?" Walter asked when they'd finished eating.

She'd found a recipe for chicken casserole and served it with homemade dinner rolls and fresh asparagus and fresh fruit salad made of seedless grapes and strawberries. For dessert she picked up a lemon torte at the local bakery that specialized in European delights.

"Summer married me full of surprises," James told his father. His eyes briefly met hers.

"What he's attempting to say is that no one knew how fertile I was, either."

"That's one of the best parts," Walter insisted. He dabbed the corner of his mouth with his napkin in a blatant effort to hide a smile.

"It certainly is one of life's more pleasant surprises," James added.

Walter's gaze grew serious as he studied her. "How are you feeling these days?"

"Wonderful."

"What's the doctor have to say?"

"That I'm in the pink of health. The baby's growing by leaps and bounds. I haven't felt him move yet, but..."

"Him?" James and Walter chimed in simultaneously.

"Or her," she retorted, smiling. She stood and started to clear the table.

"Let me help," James insisted.

"I'm not helpless, you know," Walter added.

Both men leapt from their chairs to assist her.

"Go have your coffee," Summer told the pair. "It'll only take me a few minutes to finish the dishes."

Walter looked to his son as if he wasn't sure. "There's a number of things I need to discuss with James," her father-in-law admitted.

"Then off with you," she said, and shooed them out of the kitchen.

James poured two cups of coffee and carried them into the living-room area. He paused in the doorway and looked over his shoulder. "You're sure?"

"James, honestly, go talk to your father."

Although she didn't know Walter well, it seemed to her that something was on his mind. Throughout the meal she'd noticed the way Walter studied his son. James was acting odd, too, come to think of it.

Walter wanted to discuss the campaign, but every time the elder Wilkens had introduced the subject, James expertly changed it. He did it cleverly and in such a way that it was barely noticeable. Walter had noticed, however, and after a while Summer had, too.

She ran tap water to rinse off the dinner plates and when she turned off the faucet she heard the tail end of James's comment.

"...Summer doesn't know."

She hesitated. Apparently the two men didn't realize how well their voices carried. She didn't mean to eavesdrop, but by the same token it seemed only fair that she listen, since she was the topic of conversation.

"What do you plan to do about it?" his father asked.

It took James a long time to answer. "I don't know."

"Have you tried reasoning with him?"

"No," James answered bitterly. "The man claimed he had grave doubts about my judgment. He's insulted me, insulted my wife. I don't need Southworth with an attitude like that."

"But you will need a campaign manager."

"Yes," James admitted reluctantly.

So that was what this was all about. Summer leaned against the kitchen counter and closed her eyes. Ralph had resigned, and from what evidence she'd seen on James's part, he had, too. Resigned to losing, even before the election. This didn't sound like James.

"What's the problem?" Walter asked as if reading Summer's mind. For Ralph to question James's judgment, it must have been a doozy.

James lowered his voice substantially, and Summer had to strain to hear him. "He disapproves of Summer."

"What?" Walter had no such compunction about keeping quiet. "The man's crazy."

"I've made a series of mistakes in all this," James admitted reluctantly.

"Mistakes?"

"With Summer."

The world collapsed, like a house falling in on itself, for Summer. She struggled toward a chair and literally fell into the seat.

"I should never have married her the way I did," James elaborated. "I cheated her out of the wedding she deserved. I don't know if her mother's forgiven me yet. The last I heard, her family's planning a reception after the November election. By then the baby will be here, and frankly it seems a little after the fact."

"You can't blame Summer for that."

"I don't," James remarked tartly. "I blame myself. In retrospect I realize I was afraid of losing her. So I insisted upon the marriage before she could change her mind."

"I don't understand what all of this has to do with Ralph," Walter muttered.

"Ralph believes Summer's too young for me."

"Nonsense."

"He also seems to think I've done myself a good deal of harm by not letting everyone know I was married right away. Bringing Summer here to live with me now, pregnant and insisting we've been married all along, is much too convenient to be believed.''

"It's the truth."

"You and I know that, but apparently there's already been some speculation."

"So? People will always talk. Let them, son. But you've got to do something about getting this campaign organized. There are worse things you can be accused of than marrying in secret or getting Summer pregnant before your wedding day. As far as I'm concerned, Southworth's looking for excuses."

"I refuse to subject Summer to that kind of speculation," James insisted.

"Have you talked this over with her?"

"No," James admitted reluctantly.

"You haven't?"

"I know, I know." The same defeatist attitude was back in James's voice. "I've put it off longer than I should have already."

Summer didn't hear much more of the conversation between father and son. Their marriage had hurt her husband; it might have robbed him of his dreams, cheated him out of his goals.

The phone rang long before she had time to gather her thoughts. "I'll get it," she called out to James, and reached for the extension in the kitchen. Her hand trembled as she lifted the receiver from its cradle.

"Hello," she managed, her voice uneven and weak.

"Hello," came the soft feminine reply. "You don't know me. My name's Christy Manning Franklin."

"Christy...Manning?" Summer said, stunned. She hadn't recovered from one shock before she was hit with another. This one as great as the first. "Just a moment and I'll get James."

"No, please. It's you I want to talk to."

"Me?"

"From your reaction, I'd guess that James mentioned me."

"Yes." Summer slumped down into a chair and closed her eyes. "You and James were engaged at one time."

"That's right. I understand you and James recently married?"

"Three months ago," Summer said, and was amazed by how weak her voice was. James's conversation with his father had upset her more than she realized.

"I hope you'll forgive me for being so forward. I talked it over with Cody—he's my husband—and he said since I felt so strongly about it I should phone you."

"So strongly about what?"

"About you…and James. I'll always regret the way I treated James. He deserved better, but I was younger then and weak. At one time I thought I was in love with him. I knew he loved me, and my family thought the world of him. Then I met Cody." She hesitated. "I didn't phone to tell you all this. I'm sure James filled in the details."

"Why did you call?" Summer was sure that under other circumstances she might have liked Christy Franklin.

"I wanted to tell you how very pleased I am that James found someone to love. I know it's presumptuous of me but I wanted to ask a favor of you."

"A favor." The woman had a lot of nerve.

"Love him with all your heart, Summer. James is a special, special man and he deserves a woman who'll stand by his side and love him."

"I do," she admitted softly.

"For a long time I despaired James would never marry. I can't tell you how pleased I was when Mom phoned to tell me Rich and Jamie had met you. Cody and I want to extend our very best wishes to you both."

"Thank you."

"I realize it's a lot to ask of you, but I do hope you'll keep Cody and me in mind when you count your friends. There's a special place in my heart for James. He's been a friend to our family for years. He was a tremendous help to Paul when Diane died, and again later when he married Leah. James helped Rich and Jamie, too, and I know he's been a friend to Jason and Charlotte, as well. We're all indebted to him one way or another."

"I do love him so much." She was fighting back tears and not exactly sure what she was weeping about. The fact Ralph Southworth had resigned as James's campaign manager because of her, or that James's ex-fiancée deeply cared for him.

Summer had just replaced the receiver when James stepped into the kitchen. He stood with one hand on the door.

"Who was that on the phone?" he asked.

Summer met his look straight on, waiting to read any emotion. "Christy Franklin."

"Christy?" he repeated. "What did she want?" He looked more surprised than anything.

"She called to give us her and Cody's best wishes. She said it was high time you married and that she can hardly wait to meet me."

"Really?"

"Really."

"And what did you tell her?"

Summer grinned. "I said she's to keep her cotton-pickin' hands off my husband."

James chuckled, seeming to take delight in her possessive attitude. "You aren't going to get much of an argument out of me."

"Good thing," she said, and looped her arm around his waist. Together they joined his father.

"I don't understand it," Summer muttered, and sucked in her tummy in order to button her skirt. "I can barely zip this up. It fit fine just last week."

"Honey, you're pregnant," James said matter-of-factly.

"Three months. I'm not supposed to show yet."

"You're not?" James's eyes left the mirror. His face was smeared white with shaving cream. His eyes carefully examined her rounded tummy.

"Tell me true, James. If you were meeting me for the first time, would you guess that I was pregnant?"

Her husband frowned. "This isn't one of those trick questions, is it?"

"No. I want the truth."

"All right," he said, and cleared his throat. He seemed to know intuitively that she wasn't going to like the answer. "You look pregnant to me. But then you are pregnant, so I don't understand what the big deal is."

"I'm fat already," she said, and felt like breaking into tears.

" 'Fat' is not the word I'd use to describe you."

"If I'm already showing at three months, can you just imagine what I'll look like at nine?"

His grin revealed pride and love. "I'd say you'd resemble the most beautiful woman in the world."

"No wonder I love you so much," she told her husband, and turned back to the closet. She sorted through the hangers, dismissing first one outfit and then another.

"Where are you going that you're so worried about how you look?" James asked as he turned back to face the mirror.

Summer froze. "An appointment." She prayed he didn't question her further. She'd called and arranged a meeting with Ralph Southworth, but she didn't want James to know what she'd done.

"Don't forget tonight," he reminded her absently. "We're going to the Mannings' for dinner."

"I won't forget," she promised. "Eric and Elizabeth, right?"

"Right. Knowing Elizabeth, she'll probably spend the entire day cooking. I've talked to her no less than five times in the last week. She's anxious to meet you."

"I'm anxious to meet them, too." But not nearly as anxious as she was about this meeting with Southworth. In setting up the appointment, Summer hoped to achieve several objectives. Mainly she was looking to have Ralph agree to manage James's campaign. She wanted to prove to James that he didn't need to protect her from gossip and speculation.

James left for court shortly after he finished shaving. Summer changed into the outfit, a soft gray business suit, that best disguised her pregnancy. She ran a few errands and arrived at Ralph's office at the Seattle Bank ten minutes ahead of their one-o'clock appointment.

She announced her name to the receptionist and was escorted into Southworth's office a few minutes later.

Ralph Southworth stood when she entered the room. He looked none too pleased to see her.

"Hello again," she said brightly, and claimed the chair across from his desk. She wanted it understood that she wouldn't be easily dissuaded.

"Hello," he responded stiffly.

"I hope you don't object to my making an appointment to see you. I'm afraid I may have misled your secretary into thinking it had to do with a loan."

"I see. Are you in the habit of misleading people?"

"Not at all," she assured him with a cordial smile, "but there are times when a little inventive thinking is worth five frustrating phone calls."

Southworth didn't agree or disagree with her.

"I'll get to the point of my visit," she said, not wanting to waste time. His or hers.

"Please do."

"I'd like to know the reason you've resigned as my husband's campaign manager."

Southworth rolled a pencil between his palms and avoided eye contact. "I believe that's between James and me and has nothing to do with you."

"That isn't the way I understand it," she said, grateful that he'd opened the conversation for her. "I overheard James and his father talking recently, and James said differently."

"So you eavesdrop, as well?"

He was certainly eager to tally her less than sterling characteristics.

"Yes, but in this case, I'm glad I did because I learned that you'd resigned because of me."

Southworth hesitated. "Not exactly. I questioned James's judgment."

"About our marriage?" she pressed.

Once again he seemed inclined to dodge the subject. "I don't really think..."

"I do, Mr. Southworth. This election is extremely important to James. You're extremely important to him. When he first mentioned your name to me, he said he felt you were the best man for the job."

"I am the best man for the job." The banker certainly didn't lack confidence in his abilities. "I also know a losing battle when I see it."

"Why's that?" Summer queried.

"Mrs. Wilkens, please."

"Please what, Mr. Southworth? Tell me why you question James's judgment. Until he married me, you were ready to lend him your full support. I can assure you, I'll stay exactly where I am until I have the answers to these questions." She raised her chin a stubborn half inch and refused to budge.

"If you insist..."

"I do," she told him stiffly.

"First off you're years younger than James."

"Eight years is hardly that much age difference. This is a weak excuse and unworthy of you. I do happen to look young for my age, but I can assure you I'm twenty-eight, and James is only thirty-six."

"There's also the fact you're a show girl."

"I'm an actress and singer," she countered. "Since I worked the last couple of years at Disneyland, I hardly think you can fault my morals."

"Morals is another issue entirely."

"Obviously," she said, finding she disliked this man more every time he opened his mouth. It seemed to her that Ralph Southworth was inventing excuses, none of which amounted to a hill of proverbial beans.

"You're pregnant."

"Yes. So?"

"So...it's clear to me, at least, that you and James conveniently decided to marry when you recognized your condition."

Summer laughed. "That's not true, and even if it were, all I need do is produce our marriage certificate, which I just happen to have with me." Somehow or other she knew it would boil down to this. She opened her purse and removed the envelope and handed it to the man whom her husband had once counted as his friend.

Southworth briefly read over the data and returned it to her. "I don't understand why the two of you found it necessary to marry. No one meets in Vegas, falls in love and gets married all within a few short days. Not unless they've got something to hide."

"We're in love."

"Please, Mrs. Wilkens, I've known James for a good many years. There had to be a reason other than the one you're giving me for James to have married you."

"He loved me. Isn't that good enough for you?"

Southworth looked bored with the conversation. "Then there's the fact he kept the marriage a secret."

Summer had no answer for that question. "I can't answer that, simply because I don't know why James didn't tell anyone about the wedding. My guess is that he's a private man and considers his personal life his own."

"How far along is the pregnancy?" he asked, ignoring her answer.

"Three months," she told him.

"Three months? I don't claim to know much about women and babies, but I've had several women work for me here at the bank over the years. Several of them have had babies. You easily look five or six months along."

"That's ridiculous. I know when I got pregnant."

"Do you, now?"

Summer drew in her breath and held it for several moments in an effort to contain her temper. She loved James and believed in him, but she refused to be insulted.

"I can see that we aren't going to accomplish anything here," she said sadly. "You've already formed your opinion about James and me."

"About you, Mrs. Wilkens. It's unfortunate, really. James would have made an excellent superior court judge. There's been far too much speculation about him lately. It started with the black eye. People don't want a man on the bench who can't hold on to his own temper. A judge should be above any hint of moral weakness."

"James is one of the most morally upright men I know," she insisted heatedly. "I take it as a personal insult to my husband for you to say otherwise."

"I find your loyalty to James touching, but it's too little, too late."

"What do you mean by that?" Summer demanded.

"You want your husband to win the election, don't you?"

"Yes. Of course." The question was ludicrous.

"If I were to tell you that you could make a difference, perhaps even sway the election, would you listen?"

"I'd listen," she agreed, though beyond that was something else.

Southworth stood and walked over to the window with a panoramic view of the Seattle skyline. His back was to her, and for several minutes he said nothing. He seemed to be carefully weighing his words.

"You've already admitted that I'm the best man to run James's campaign."

"Yes," she said reluctantly, not as willing to admit it as she had been when she first arrived.

"I can help win him this September's primary and the November election. Don't discount the political sway I have in this community, Mrs. Wilkens. It's substantial."

Summer said nothing.

"When James first mentioned that he'd married you, I suggested that he keep you out of the picture until after the election."

"I see."

"I did this for a number of important reasons, all of which James opted to ignore."

"He...he really wasn't given much choice," she felt obligated to tell him. "I turned up on his doorstep, suitcase in hand."

Ralph nodded as if he'd long suspected this had been the case. "I can turn James's campaign around if you'd agree to one thing."

Her stomach tightened, knowing before the words were voiced what was about to be said. "Yes?"

"Simply disappear for several months. Stay out of the picture, and once the November election is over, you can move back into his house. It won't matter then."

She closed her eyes and lowered her head. "I see."

"Will you do it?"

"Summer, I'm sorry I'm late." James kissed her soundly and rushed up the stairs to change clothes.

He was late? She hadn't noticed. Since her meeting with Ralph Southworth, Summer had spent what remained of the afternoon in a stupor. She felt numb and sad. Tears lay just beneath the surface, ready to break free.

The decision should have been far less difficult than she was finding it to be. She could give her husband the dream he'd always wanted or ruin his life.

Five minutes later James returned. He'd changed out of his suit and tie and wore slacks and a shirt and sweater. "Are you ready?" he asked.

"Ready?" She didn't know what he was talking about.

"The dinner tonight with the Mannings. Remember?"

"Of course," she said, forcing a smile. How could she have forgotten that? James was like a schoolboy eager to show off his science project. Only in this case, she was the project.

He escorted her out the front door and into the car that was parked in front of the house. "You haven't had much campaigning to do lately," she commented.

"I know."

"What's Ralph have to say?" she asked, wanting to know how much he was willing to tell her.

"Not much. Let's not talk about the election tonight, all right?"

"Why not?" she pressed.

"I don't want to have to think about it. These people are my longtime friends. They're like a second set of parents to me."

"Do they know I'm pregnant?"

"No, but I won't need to tell them, will I?" His hand gently patted her abdomen.

"James," she whispered, barely understanding why it was important that he know this now. "When we get home this evening, I want to make love."

His gaze briefly left the road. "All right."

The emptiness inside could only be filled with his love.

"Are you all right, darling?"

She forced herself to smile and laid her head against his shoulder. "Of course."

"Something's different."

"It is?" Just that her heart felt as if it had been chopped in half. Just that she'd never felt so cold or alone in her life. Southworth had asked her to turn her back on the man she loved. He'd asked that she leave and do it in such a way that he wouldn't follow. He'd asked that she bear her child alone.

When they arrived at the Manning family home, James parked the car and turned to Summer. He studied her for an intense moment. "I love you."

"I love you," she whispered in return. She felt incredibly close to tears.

James helped her out of the car. They walked to the front porch, and her husband rang the doorbell. When she wasn't looking, he stole a kiss.

A distinguished-looking older gentleman opened the door for them. "James, by heaven, it's good to see you again."

"Eric, this is my wife, Summer."

"Hello, Summer." Instead of shaking her hand, Eric Manning gently hugged her.

They stepped inside, and all at once, from behind every available hiding space, people appeared.

They were greeted with an unanimous chorus of "Surprise."

Chapter Eleven

Summer didn't understand what was happening. All at once a large number of strange people surrounded her. People with happy faces, people who looked delighted to be meeting her.

"Elizabeth," James protested. "What have you done?"

The middle-aged woman hugged first James and then Summer. "You know how much I love a party," she told him, grinning broadly. "What better excuse than to meet your wife. I'm the mother of this brood," she told Summer proudly. Her gaze scanned the room. There were men, women and children milling about. "You must be Summer."

"I am. You must be Elizabeth."

"Indeed I am."

Before she could protest, Summer was lured away from James's side. The men seemed eager to talk to

James alone. Summer looked longingly to her husband and him to her, then he grinned and followed his friends into the family room.

Soon Summer found herself in the kitchen, which bustled with activity. "I'm Jamie. We met the other day in the restaurant," Rich's wife reminded her.

"I remember," Summer told her, stepping out of the way of a youngster racing past her at breakneck speed.

"These two women with the openly curious looks on their faces are my two sisters-in-law. The first one here," Jamie said, looping her arm around the woman who was obviously pregnant, "is Charlotte. She's married to Jason. He's the real slob of the family."

"But he's getting better," Charlotte told her.

"When's your baby due?"

"July," Charlotte told her. "This is our second. Doug's asleep. I also have a daughter from my first marriage, but Carrie's working and couldn't be here. I'm sure you'll get the chance to meet her later."

"Our baby is due in September," Summer said, ending speculation.

The women exchanged glances. "You're barely four months pregnant?"

Miserable, Summer nodded. "I think something must be wrong. The first couple of months I was terribly sick. I'm much better now that I'm in Seattle with James. But my figure's ballooning. Few of my clothes fit anymore."

"It happens like that sometimes," Elizabeth said with the voice of experience. "I showed more with Paul, my first, than I did with Christy, my youngest. Don't ask me why nature plays these silly tricks on us women. One would think we had enough to put up with dealing with men."

A chorus of agreement followed.

Elizabeth lifted the hors d'oeuvre platter out of the refrigerator. "The good news is I was blessed with three wonderful sons. The bad news is I was blessed with three wonderful sons. My daughters are an entirely different story."

"I don't know what to think with this baby," Summer told everyone, and pressed her hand over her stomach. "We didn't plan to have me get pregnant so soon."

"I bet James is thrilled."

Summer smiled and nodded. "We both are."

"This is Leah," Jamie said, introducing her other sister-in-law. "She's Paul's wife. Paul's the author in the family."

"He's very good," Leah said proudly. "His first book was published last year, and he's sold two more."

"That's great."

"Let me help," Jamie insisted, and lifted the platter out of Elizabeth's hands. He carried it over to the long table, which was beautifully decorated with paper bells and a lovely ceramic bride-and-groom centerpiece.

"I've been waiting for a good long time to use these decorations," Elizabeth announced disparagingly. "Unfortunately my children gave me little opportunity. It all started with the girls. Neither one of them saw fit to have a church wedding. Then Rich married Jamie and Paul married Leah, again without the fancy wedding the way I always wanted."

"Jason and Charlotte were the only ones to have a big wedding," Leah explained. "I don't think Eric and Elizabeth have ever forgiven the rest of us."

"You're darn right, we haven't," Eric said, joining them.

"They made it up to us with grandchildren, dear," his wife interjected. "Now, don't get started on that. We're more fortunate than words can say."

Summer couldn't remember the last time she'd sat down at a dinner table with this many people. A rowdy group of children ate at a card table set up in the kitchen. Twin boys seemed to head up the dissension and took delight in teasing their younger cousins. The noise level was something else, but Summer didn't mind.

More than once she found James's gaze watching her. She smiled and silently conveyed that she was enjoying herself. Who wouldn't?

There were gifts to open following the meal, and plenty of marital advice. Summer, whose mood had been bleak earlier, found herself laughing so hard her sides hurt.

The evening was an unqualified success, and afterward Summer felt as if she'd found a house full of new friends. Jamie, Leah and Charlotte seemed eager to make her feel welcome. Charlotte was the first to extend an invitation for lunch. Since they were both pregnant, Summer felt they already shared common ground.

"A week from Friday," Charlotte reminded her when Summer was ready to leave. She mentioned the name of the restaurant and wrote out her phone number on the back of a business card for Summer.

"I'll look forward to it," Summer told her, and meant it.

It wasn't until they were home that Summer remembered her meeting with Southworth. She didn't know if she'd be in Seattle in another week, let alone available for lunch.

A heavy sadness pressed against her heart.

James slipped his arm around her waist. He turned off the downstairs lights, and together they moved toward the stairs. "As I recall," he whispered, nibbling on her earlobe, "you made me a promise earlier."

"I did?"

"You asked me to make love to you, remember?"

Shivers of awareness scooted up and down her backbone. "I did?"

"I certainly hope you intend to live up to your part of the bargain."

"Me?" she questioned, and then yawned loudly. She placed her hand in front of her mouth, fighting back waves of tiredness. "I have no intention of changing my mind."

"Good." They reached the top of the stairs, and he nuzzled her neck. "I wonder if it will always be like this?" he murmured, steering her toward their bedroom.

"Always be like what?"

"My desire for you. I feel like a kid in a candy store."

"I will say one thing," Summer said, smiling up at her husband, "the last place you're a stuffed shirt is in the bedroom."

James chuckled.

Summer yawned again. "I enjoyed meeting the Mannings. They're wonderful people."

"Are you telling me something?" he asked.

She nodded. "I'm tired, James." But it was more than being physically weary. Summer experienced a mental exhaustion that was bone deep.

"Come on, love," James urged gently. He led her into the bedroom and between long, soul-deep kisses, he undressed her and gently laid her on the bed. He tucked her in and tenderly kissed her cheek.

The light dimmed, and Summer snuggled into the warmth. It took her a few moments to realize James hadn't joined her.

"James?" She forced her eyes open.

"Yes, love."

"Aren't you coming to bed?"

"In a few minutes," he promised. "I'm taking a shower first."

A shower, she mused, wondering at his sudden penchant for cleanliness.

Then she heard him add in a half-muted tone, "A nice, long cold shower."

James had been looking forward to the ultrasound appointment for weeks. He'd met Dr. Wise, Summer's obstetrician, earlier and had immediately liked and trusted the man, who was in his late forties. David Wise had been delivering babies for more than twenty years, and his calm reassurance had gone a long way toward answering James's worries.

Summer sat next to him in the waiting room, her features pale and lifeless. She hadn't been herself in the past few days, and James wondered what could be troubling her. He didn't want to pry and hoped she'd soon share whatever plagued her.

They held hands and silently waited until Summer's name was announced.

Within a few minutes they were called and led into the examination room. It was all James could manage to sit still and wait for Dr. Wise to explain the procedure.

Summer was instructed to lie flat on her back on the examining table. Her top was peeled open to expose the small roundness that was their child. James smiled down on her while Dr. Wise explained the process.

A gel was spread across Summer's smooth tummy. It must have been cold, because she flinched.

"It's about this time that several women suggest the male of the species should be responsible for childbearing," Dr. Wise told him.

"No, thanks," James said, "I like my role in all this just fine."

Dr. Wise chuckled. He pressed a stereoscope-like instrument across Summer's stomach. Everyone's attention turned toward the monitor.

For his part James was terribly disappointed. This wasn't like any picture he'd ever seen. The monitor resembled a television screen badly in need of a cable hookup. No matter how hard he looked, he couldn't make out a single detail.

"There's the baby's head," Dr. Wise said, pointing to a curved shape on the screen.

James squinted and he noticed Summer was doing the same. Apparently she was having as much trouble as he was identifying their child.

"Well, look at this," the physician continued, sounding pleasantly surprised.

"At what?" James intently studied the screen.

"We have a second little head."

"My baby has two heads," Summer cried in alarm, lifting her head.

"Two heads," James echoed, his heart in his throat. "Something's wrong."

"What I'm saying," Dr. Wise returned calmly, "is that there appears to be two babies."

"Twins?"

"It certainly looks that way." Dr. Wise moved the instrument across Summer's abdomen. "Here's the first head," he said, pointing out the barely discernible round curve in the blurred, snow-filled picture, "and here's the second."

James squinted for all he was worth just to find the one. "Twins," he muttered.

"That explains a good deal," Dr. Wise said, and gently patted Summer's arm. "I'll run a copy of this for you both," he said, and pushed a series of buttons.

Within a matter of minutes they had the readout to examine for themselves. While Summer dressed, James studied the fuzzy picture that resembled a sonar reading. Circular lines outlined the picture.

"Twins," he said aloud, just for the pleasure of hearing himself say the word. Summer appeared just then, and he stood and smiled broadly. "Twins," he repeated, grinning ear to ear. Had they been someplace else, he might have clicked his heels.

She smiled, and James thought he saw tears in her eyes.

"It won't be so bad," he said, then immediately regretted his lack of sensitivity. He wasn't the one carrying two babies, nor would he be the one delivering the twins. "I'll do whatever I can to help," he hurried to reassure her.

She gave him a watery smile.

"Say something," he pleaded. "Are you happy?"

"I don't know," she admitted. "I'm still in shock. What about you?"

"I've rarely been more pleased about anything in my life. I can hardly wait to tell my father. He's going to be absolutely delighted."

Summer looked at the ultrasound. "Can you tell? Boys? Girls? One of each?"

James scratched the side of his head. "I had enough trouble finding the two heads. I decided not to try to decipher anything else."

They left the doctor's office and headed for the parking garage across the street.

"This calls for a celebration. I'll take you to lunch," he suggested.

"I was thinking more along the lines of a nap."

James grinned and looked at his watch. "Is there time?"

"James," she said, and laughed softly. "I meant a real nap. I'm exhausted."

"Oh." Disappointment shot through him. "You don't want to celebrate with a fancy lunch?"

She shook her head. "Don't be upset with me. I guess I need time to think everything through."

That sounded odd to James. What, after all, was there to think about? True, Summer was pregnant with twins, but they had plenty of time to prepare for the happy event. As for any mental readjustment needed, well, he'd made that in all of two seconds. It shouldn't take her much longer than that. The twins were a surprise, yes, but a pleasant one.

"This news has really upset you, hasn't it?" he asked.

"No," she was quick to assure him. "It's just that...well, it changes things."

"What things?"

She shook her head and didn't answer. James frowned, not knowing how to calm her fears or answer her doubts. She didn't seem to look to him for either and instead appeared to be drawing into herself.

"You don't mind if I tell my dad, do you?" he asked. If he didn't share the news with someone soon, he was afraid he'd be reduced to stopping strangers on the street and announcing it.

She smiled softly at him, her eyes alight with love. "I don't mind if you tell Walter."

He walked her to where she'd parked and kissed her, then walked the short distance back to the King County Courthouse. His thoughts were so full of Summer that he went a block too far before he realized what he'd done.

When he was in his office, the first thing he did was reach for the phone.

His father answered almost immediately. "You'll never guess what I'm looking at," he told Walter.

"You're right, I'll never guess."

"Today was Summer's ultrasound," James reminded him. Hiding his excitement was becoming more and more difficult.

"Ah, yes, and what did you learn?"

James could hear the eagerness in Walter's voice. "I have the picture of the ultrasound with me."

"And?" Walter prodded.

"I'm staring at the picture of your grandchildren right this moment."

"Boy or girl?"

James couldn't help it. He laughed. "You didn't listen very well."

"I did, too, and I want to know what do we have? A boy or a girl?"

"Could be one of each," James informed him primly. "I'm having a hard enough time making much out of this. It takes more knowledgeable eyes than mine to decipher this snow."

"Twins," Walter shouted. "You mean to say Summer's having twins?"

"That's what I'm telling you."

"Well, I'll be! Hot dog, boy, this is good news."

James couldn't remember a time Walter had sounded more excited. For that matter, he was delighted himself.

It isn't every day a man learns he's about to be a father two times over. Discovering the truth the first time had come as a surprise, but this . . . this news was too good to hold inside. He felt as if he was about to burst the buttons right off his shirt.

Summer didn't go directly home. Instead, she found herself driving around, mulling over the situation between her and James. She loved him so much. The thought of leaving him, even when she knew it was the best thing for his career, left her with a heavy heart.

What she wanted was to talk to her mother, but her parents were vacationing with friends and were touring the south in their motor home. They weren't due back for another month. Summer received postcards every other day with the latest updates and a list of their adventures.

It did the parents good to get away, Summer thought, but she really needed her mother right now.

Without realizing she knew the way, Summer drove to the Manning family home. She parked and mulled over whether she was doing the right thing by dropping by without warning.

It took her a full five minutes to gather up enough nerve to climb out of the car, walk up to the steps and ring the bell.

Elizabeth Manning answered the door herself. Her face lit up with warmth. "Summer, what a pleasant surprise."

"I hope I haven't come at an inconvenient time."

"Not at all," Elizabeth said, and stepped aside. "I was mixing meatballs. Eric loves his meat-a-balls," she said in a heavy Italian accent. "It's his bowling day, so he's out just now. Can I get you a cup of coffee or something?"

"No, thank you."

Elizabeth sat down in the living room.

"Would it be all right if we talked in the kitchen?" Summer asked after an awkward moment.

"Of course."

"I . . . I realize you barely know me, and it's an imposition for me to pop in out of the blue like this."

"It's no problem. I'm delighted to see you again."

"I . . . my parents have a motor home," Summer said, wishing now she'd thought matters through more carefully before she approached James's friends. "They're traveling across the south now."

"Eric and I do quite a bit of traveling in our own motor home. We visit Christy and her sister Taylor at least once a year. We're getting to where Montana's like a second home to us." She dug her hands deep into the bowl of hamburger and removed a golf-ball-size hunk of meat. Expertly she formed it into a perfect round shape.

"Basically I wanted to thank you for everything you did the other night for James and me," Summer said.

When it came right down to it, she realized she couldn't burden this woman with her troubles. She would have welcomed the advice, but felt awkward spilling out her heart to a woman who was little more than a stranger to her.

"When you know me better, you'll learn that I'll use any excuse for a party. James has always been a special friend to our family, and we couldn't be more pleased to learn that he'd married."

"I didn't know it was possible to love anyone so much," she confessed, and then because tears began to leak from the corners of her eyes, Summer abruptly stood. "Listen, I should go, but thank you. I'll see myself to the door."

"Summer," Elizabeth called after her. "Summer, is everything all right?"

Summer was in her car by the time Elizabeth appeared in the doorway. She hurriedly started the engine and pulled away, certain that she'd done far more harm than good in her impromptu visit.

Wiping the tears from her eyes, Summer drove home. She walked into the house and up the stairs, where she lay down on the bed and briefly closed her eyes.

She had to leave, but she didn't know where she'd go. If she didn't do it soon, she'd never find the courage. Only minutes earlier she declared to James's family friend how deeply she loved her husband. That being the case, doing what was best for him shouldn't be nearly this difficult.

But it was.

Sobbing and miserable, Summer got up from the bed and pulled out one big suitcase from the closet. She packed what she thought she would need and carried it down to the car.

At the last minute she decided she couldn't leave without writing James. She sat at his desk for several moments in an effort to compose a letter that would explain what she was doing and why. But it was all so complicated, and in the end she simply said he was better off without her and penned her name. She re-read it twice before tucking it inside an envelope.

Tears streamed down her cheeks, and she rubbed away the moisture. It wouldn't be so bad, she attempted to convince herself. The babies would be less than two months old when the election was over, and then she'd be free to return.

That is if James wanted her back.

James had seldom been in a better mood. He sat in the courtroom, convinced he wore a grin a Cheshire cat would envy.

His secretary didn't know what to think of him. During a brief recess, he waltzed back to the office to phone Summer, whistling as he went.

His wife might not have wanted to celebrate with lunch, but their news deserved some sort of festivities. Dinner at the Space Needle. A night on the town.

While he was in his office, he decided to have flowers delivered to the house with a card that said she'd made him the happiest man alive. Twice. Let the florist make what he would of that.

The phone rang four times before the answering machine kicked in. James hung up rather than leave a message. He'd try to call again later. Summer was probably resting. He hoped the phone hadn't disturbed her.

"Judge Wilkens?" Mrs. Jamison, his secretary, stopped him.

"Yes?"

"Your father phoned earlier. He wanted me to let you know he's been to the toy store and purchased two giant teddy bears. He asked me to tell you he'll be dropping them off at the house around six this evening. Also he said something about having made dinner reservations in case you hadn't thought of that."

"Great." James chuckled. So his father couldn't hold back his delight, either. He laughed again and discovered his secretary staring at him blankly.

"See this," James said, taking the ultrasound picture from the inside of his suit pocket. He was so damn proud one would think it was an Olympic gold medal. "My wife and I just learned we're having twins."

"Your wife? Twins for you and Summer. Why, Your Honor..." Her mouth resembled that of a trout out of water, but she recovered quickly. "Congratulations."

"Thank you," James said, and then, looking at his watch, he hurried back into the courtroom.

The afternoon was sure to be hectic. James was hearing the sad case of a man who, crazed on drugs and alcohol, had gone on a shooting rampage. He'd killed three people and injured seventeen more. The case was just getting under way but was sure to attract a lot of media attention. James knew the defense was hinging its case on a plea of temporary insanity.

A door opened in the back of the courtroom. James was busy and didn't look up. Out of the corner of his eye, he saw a lone figure slip into the back row. Whoever it was apparently didn't want to be recognized. She wore a scarf and large, oval sunglasses.

Twice more James found his gaze returning to the figure in the back of the courtroom. If he didn't know better he'd think it was Summer.

Whoever it was stayed for a fair amount of time. An hour or longer. He didn't know when the woman left, but James couldn't keep from being curious.

He guessed the woman was a reporter. The newspeople were already attracted to the sensationalism of the trial, and it was sure to generate its share of coverage.

When he was finished for the afternoon, James returned to his office and removed his robe. His secretary brought in a stack of phone messages. The one that seemed the most peculiar was from Elizabeth Manning. She'd never phoned him at court. Generally she contacted him at home.

Leaning back in his chair, he reached for the phone. "Hello, Elizabeth," he said cheerfully. It was on the tip of his tongue to tell her his and Summer's good news, but she cut him off.

"You best tell me what's wrong. I'll have you know I've been worried sick all afternoon."

"Worried? About what?"

"You and Summer."

Sometimes Christy's mother baffled him. "I don't have a clue what you're talking about. I will tell you Summer and I were at the doctor's this morning and learned she's pregnant with twins."

The words fell into an empty silence.

"That can't be it," Elizabeth mulled aloud. "She was here, you know."

"Who?"

"Summer," Elizabeth answered shortly.

"When?"

"This afternoon. Listen to me, James, there's something terribly wrong. I knew it the minute I saw that girl. She was upset and close to tears. At first I thought you two might have had an argument."

"No..." James frowned. "What did she say?"

"Something about her parents traveling in their motor home. I suppose I should have realized then she was looking to talk something out with me, but like a fool, I started chattering about Eric and I visiting the girls every year. I was hoping she'd relax enough to speak her mind."

"Tell me everything that happened."

"Well, first off, Summer started to cry and did a real poor job of hiding her tears. They seemed to pour out of her eyes. The dear girl is hurting something terrible."

"Go on," James urged.

"She said she'd come to thank me for the party, which we both knew was an excuse. Then she apparently changed her mind about talking with me. Before I could stop her, she was gone."

"Gone? What do you mean gone?"

"The dear girl literally ran out of the house. I tried to catch up with her, but with my bum leg, that was impossible. I'm not as young as I used to be."

"She drove off without a word more?"

"That's right." Elizabeth sounded flustered and concerned. "What could be wrong, James?"

"I don't know. I simply don't know. She seemed all right this morning." Or had she been? James didn't know anymore. "I'll give you a call this evening," James assured his friend. "I'm sure everything's going to be fine."

"I do hope you're right. Summer was very upset, James. That's odd...."

"What is?"

"I remember something else she said, and now that I think about it, it was after she told me this that she started to weep."

"What was it?" James asked anxiously.

"She told me how much she loved you."

A few minutes later, when he'd finished speaking to Elizabeth, James was more confused than ever. He tried contacting Summer once more, but again there was no answer. He left the office abruptly, without a word to his staff.

When he got to the house he burst through the front door. "Summer," he shouted, his heart racing.

He was greeted with only silence. He raced up the stairs, taking two at a time. He searched every room but didn't find her.

What confused him further was that her clothes hung in her closet, but one suitcase was missing. One would think if she was planning to leave him, that she would have taken more things with her. The only items James could find missing were her toothbrush, slippers and a book she'd been religiously studying that had to do with pregnancy and birth.

Baffled, James wandered back downstairs. He scouted out the kitchen and the other rooms. The last place he looked was in his den. There he found an envelope propped against the base of the lamp.

James sat down and tore open the letter. It was brief, and as far as he could see, it made no sense. All he understood was that she'd left him. He hadn't a clue why, other than that she seemed to think she was doing what was best for him.

A sick feeling attacked his stomach. He sat there longer than he realized. The next thing he knew the doorbell chimed. He didn't get up to answer, and a couple of minutes later the door opened on its own and his father stepped into the house.

"You might have let me in," he grumbled, and set one huge teddy bear in the chair across from James. "I'll be back in a jiffy," his father informed him. He returned a couple of minutes later with the second stuffed bear.

"How did you get in?" James asked, his voice devoid of emotion.

"You gave me a key, remember?"

He didn't.

"What's going on around here?" Walter asked. "One would think you were attending a funeral. Where's my daughter-in-law who's giving me twin grandchildren?"

"Apparently Summer has decided to leave me. She's gone."

Chapter Twelve

"Gone," Walter protested, "what do you mean Summer's gone?"

"Gone, Dad," James said bitterly, "as in packed-a-suitcase-and-walked-out-the-door gone."

His father quickly sat down. "But why?"

James couldn't answer that any more than he could his own plaguing questions. He handed Walter the brief letter Summer had left him.

Walter read it over, then raised questioning eyes to James. "What's this supposed to mean?"

"Your guess is as good as mine."

"You must have said something," Walter insisted. "Think, boy, think."

"I've done nothing but think, and for the life of me none of this makes sense. I thought at first that she was upset about the news of the twins. I realize now that whatever it is has been worrying her for some time."

"What could it be?"

"I just don't know. I'd hoped she'd tell me."

"You mean to say you didn't ask?"

"No."

Walter glared at him with disbelief. "That's the first thing I learned after I married your mother. She never told me a damn thing that I didn't have to pry out of her with a crowbar. It's a man's duty, a husband's lot in life. When you didn't ask, Summer must have assumed you didn't love her."

In spite of his heavy heart, James briefly smiled. "Trust me, Dad, Summer has no fear about speaking her mind, and as for me loving her, she couldn't have doubted that. I've been half-crazy for her from the moment we met."

"She loves you." Walter's words were more statement than question.

"Yes," James agreed. He felt secure in her love. Comfortable. Confident. Or he had until now.

"Where would she go?"

This was the same question that had troubled James from the moment he discovered her letter. "I don't know."

"Have you contacted her parents?"

He would have, first thing, but it wouldn't do him any good. James rubbed a hand down his face, tired to the very marrow of his bones. "They're traveling across the Southwest in their motor home."

"What about friends she's made since the move?"

"They're more acquaintances than friends. She stopped by to volunteer two mornings a week at the library, but she's only mentioned meeting the children's librarian in passing. From what I understand, she's a middle-aged woman in her late fifties.''

"I see." Walter frowned. "What about the Mannings?"

"She stopped off to talk to Elizabeth earlier this afternoon. Elizabeth phoned me and said Summer had started to weep and then hurriedly left without saying anything more."

Walter's look became thoughtful. "She apparently tried to reach out for help."

"The only other person I could think of was her former roommate, Julie. I phoned her in Orange County and discovered she's gone on tour."

"Julie, of course," his father said as if he should have thought of her himself.

"Julie's new roommate told me her contract with Disney was up at the same time as Summer's. Now that I think about it, Summer did say something about Julie touring with a musical group, singing background."

"Then it's unlikely Summer would have any way of getting hold of her, either."

"No." James closed his eyes. His wife had walked out on him into a cold, friendless world. Whatever had driven her away must have eaten at her for days.

"Did you think to check the airlines?"

"Where would she go?" James asked, losing his patience.

"I don't know," Walter admitted reluctantly. He couldn't seem to sit still. He began pacing.

The movement soon irritated James. "For the love of heaven, will you kindly sit down?"

"I can't do nothing."

"Yes, you can and you will," James insisted, making a decision. "I'll take the car and drive around and see if I can find her. You stay here and man the phone in case she calls or we hear something."

"That sounds like a good idea. Check in with me every hour."

James nodded. As he climbed into the car, James realized it was as if he'd lost a part of himself. He had. Summer had walked away and taken with her not only his two unborn children, but his very heart.

He felt as if he were looking for a needle in the proverbial haystack as he pulled onto the narrow neighborhood street. Try as he might, he couldn't think of where she would go. He attempted to put himself in her shoes. Alone in a strange city with few friends.

The only thing James felt he could do was to ask God to guide him.

The wind blew off Puget Sound and buffeted against Summer as she stood at the end of the long pier. The waterfront was one of her favorite places in all of Seattle. Not knowing where else to instruct the taxi to take her, she'd had the driver drop her off here.

She loved to shop at the Pike Place Market. Every Saturday morning James came down to the waterfront with her, and they loaded up with fresh fruits and vegetables for the week. Taking the stairs down from First Avenue to the Seattle Aquarium, Summer had been thrilled to ride the trolley car.

James had been wonderfully patient while she browsed in the tourist shops that stretched along the waterfront. Some of their happiest moments in Seattle had been spent on this very pier. It was in a nearby restaurant that they'd met Rich and Jamie Manning that first time. It was here that Summer had felt happiest with James.

How she hated to leave. It was as if everything in her was fighting to keep her in Seattle. Her husband was here, her home, her very life.

The instant she'd walked into James's large house, she'd experienced a powerful sense of homecoming. She'd never said anything to her husband—he might think she was silly—but Summer felt as if his house had always been meant for them together.

She'd like to think that somewhere deep in James's subconscious he'd known he was going to fall in love and marry. The house had been in preparation for her coming into his life.

Tears misted her eyes. She didn't want to mull over her unhappiness. So, she turned her attention to the water. The lull of the tide fascinated her. The dark, murky waters of Elliott Bay glistened in the lights from overhead. A green-and-white ferry from one of the islands approached the terminal.

Summer closed her eyes, willing herself to turn around and walk away. Only she didn't know where she would go. One thing was certain, she couldn't spend the night standing at the end of the pier. Soon she'd need to find herself a hotel room. In the morning her head would be clearer, and she could make some basic decisions.

She was about to reach for her suitcase when she sensed someone approaching her. Not wanting company, even the nonintrusive sort, Summer turned away from the railing. She kept her gaze lowered, but even that didn't prevent her from recognizing James.

He sauntered to the railing several feet from where she was standing. Wordlessly he stared into the distance. It appeared as if he hadn't a care in the world.

Summer wasn't sure what she should do. She couldn't very well walk away from him now. It had been difficult enough the first time. She sincerely doubted she had the strength to do it again.

"How'd...how'd you know where to find me?" she asked.

He stared into the distance and didn't answer her for several moments. "Lucky guess," he said in cool tones.

Summer sincerely doubted that James felt lucky to be married to her just then. He was furious with her. More angry than she could ever remember seeing him with anyone.

Summer wanted to explain that she was an albatross hanging around his neck. That she was a detriment to his career, but she couldn't force the words through her parched throat.

The tears that had flowed most of the day returned in force. She brushed away the moisture from her face with her fingertips.

"Was I such a bad husband?" he demanded in the same chilling tone.

"No," she whispered.

"Did I do something so terrible you can't find it in your heart to forgive me?"

She shook her head and sobbed, jerking her shoulders with the force of the action.

"You've fallen out of love with me," he suggested next.

"Don't be ridiculous," she cried. If she loved him any more than she already did, she didn't think her heart could bear it.

"Then tell me what prompted you to walk out on me."

"My letter..."

"Your cryptic note explained nothing."

"I...I..." She was trembling so much, she couldn't speak.

James walked over to where she was standing and reached for her suitcase. "We're headed back to the house and we're going to talk this out. When we're finished, and if you're still set on leaving, I'll drive you to the airport myself. Understand?"

All she could manage was a meager nod.

Thankfully he'd parked the car close by. Summer felt weak and disoriented. She shouldn't be this happy that James had found her, but she was. Even if he was furious with her, she was so very grateful he was taking her home.

James opened the car door for her and set her suitcase in the back seat. On the entire ride home, he didn't speak so much as a single word.

When they pulled into the driveway, Summer noticed Walter's car.

"Your father's here?"

James didn't answer her, and really one wasn't necessary. It was obvious Walter was anxiously waiting inside.

"Where'd you find her?" he asked the instant they appeared, ignoring Summer.

"The waterfront."

"Sit down, sit down," her father-in-law insisted, guiding Summer to a chair. She felt as if she were about to collapse and must have looked it, too.

"Now tell me what the hell this is all about?" James demanded of her. His words were as rough as bits of chewed-off steel.

"You can't speak to her like that," Walter chastised. "Can't you see the poor girl's had the worst day of her life?" He directed his attention to Summer and smiled gently. "Now tell me what the hell this is all about."

Summer looked from one man to the other. "Would it be all right if I spoke to James alone?" she asked her father-in-law. She couldn't deal with both men at the same time.

It looked for a moment as if Walter wasn't going to leave. "I suppose," he agreed with heavy reluctance. "I'll be waiting in the other room."

"Walter," Summer said, stopping him on the way out the door. "I take it the two teddy bears are your doing."

He nodded sheepishly. "The car's loaded with goodies. I'm afraid I got a little carried away."

"These babies are going to love their grandpa."

Walter grinned and, when he walked out of the den, he gently closed the door.

James stood by the fireplace, his back to her. Summer suspected he was mentally preparing a list of questions. She wasn't even sure she had all the answers. She wasn't sure she wanted him to ask them.

"I . . . I went to see Ralph Southworth," she said in a voice that was reed thin.

James whirled around. "You did what?"

"I ... I overheard you and your father talking not long ago, and I learned that Southworth had resigned as your campaign manager."

"So Southworth is what this is all about," James said thoughtfully. His eyes hardened. "What happened between the two of us had nothing to do with you."

"James, please, I know otherwise. I...I knew from the start that Ralph disapproved of me. I'm not sure why, possibly because I'm an actress. It doesn't matter."

"You're damn right it doesn't. Because Southworth doesn't matter."

Summer wasn't sure she believed that. "Afterward it seemed like you'd given up on the election. In the last two weeks you haven't made a single public appearance. When I asked, you didn't want to talk about it...."

"There are things you don't know."

"Things you wouldn't tell me."

James sat across from her and leaned forward, pressing his elbows against his knees. He didn't say anything for several moments. His look was thoughtful as he rubbed the back of his neck.

"What was I supposed to think?" she cried when he didn't explain. "Being a judge is the most important thing in the world to you. You were born for this ... I couldn't take it away from you. Don't you understand?"

"You're wrong about one thing. Being a superior court judge means nothing if you're not at my side. Nothing, least of all my career, is worth losing my wife and family over."

"I was going to come back," she whispered, her gaze lowered. "After the election . . ."

"Do you mean to say you were going to deliver our babies on your own? Do you honestly think I wouldn't have turned this city upside down looking for you?"

"I . . . didn't know what to think. Southworth said . . ."

"Don't even tell me," James said, and a muscle leapt in his jaw. "I can well imagine what he told you. The man's a world-class idiot. He saw you as a liability when you're my greatest asset."

"If you truly believe that then why did you throw in the towel?"

"I haven't," he said heatedly. "I took a few days to think everything through and decide whom to ask to manage the rest of my campaign. It seems there were several who wanted the job, and, well, I didn't want to offend anyone."

"But Southworth said he could sway the election for you . . . he claims to have considerable political clout."

"He seems to think he does," James said tightly.

"We made a deal," she whispered, and lowered her gaze.

"What kind of deal?" James demanded.

"Southworth agreed to manage your campaign if I left the scene until after the election."

James snickered softly. "It's unfortunate you didn't check with me first."

"Why?"

"I don't want Southworth anywhere near my campaign."

Summer bristled. "You certainly might have said something earlier."

"True," James admitted slowly. "But I wanted everything squared away before I announced I'd changed campaign managers and why."

Her husband reached for her hands and took them in his own. "What you don't understand is that I wouldn't have taken Southworth back under any circumstances. First of all I won't allow any man to talk about my wife the way he did you. It's true I made some mistakes when we first married. I blame myself for not publishing our wedding announcement first thing. Frankly I didn't think of it."

"I didn't, either. And remember we were talking about an April ceremony in the beginning." Summer wasn't willing for him to accept all the blame.

"You're my wife, and I couldn't be more proud that someone as beautiful and talented as you would choose to marry me. Ralph made it sound as if we should keep you stuffed in a closet until after the election, which is utterly ridiculous. In looking back, I'm angry with myself for not taking a stand sooner."

"What about the election?" She didn't care to hear anything more about Southworth.

"I'll get to that in a minute. When Southworth claimed that he questioned my judgment was when I realized what a fool I'd been to have ever listened to the man."

"But—"

"Let me finish, sweetheart. The best thing I ever did in my life was marry you."

"It was impulsive and—"

"Smart," he said, cutting her off. "I don't need Southworth to win this campaign. For a time he had me convinced I did, but I know otherwise now."

"What about his political sway?"

"That's a laugh. A man who's as narrow-minded and self-righteous as Ralph Southworth can't afford the luxury of friends. He has none, but he doesn't seem to realize it. If he hadn't decided to leave my campaign, I would have been forced to ask him to resign."

It was a good thing Summer was already sitting down. "You mean to say I ripped my heart out and left you for nothing?"

"Exactly."

"Oh."

James gently gathered her in his arms. "I may be touted as one of the finest legal minds in the state, but I'm nothing without you."

Summer sobbed into his shoulder.

"Winning the election would be an empty victory if you weren't standing at my side. I want you to share that moment with me. I love you, Summer, and I love our babies, too."

"Oh, James, I've been so unhappy. I didn't know what to do."

"Don't ever leave me again. It was like a frost came over me and didn't go away until I saw you standing at the end of that pier."

Summer tightened her hold on her husband.

Walter tapped against the door. "Can I come in yet?"

"No," James growled.

"I take it you two have settled your differences."

"We're working on it," Summer called out.

"Then I think I'll leave you to your reunion."

"Good night, Dad," James murmured in what was an obvious hint for his father to leave.

"Night, kids. Kiss and make up, all right?"

"We're going to do a lot more than kiss," James whispered in her ear.

"Promises, promises, promises," she murmured.

"You can bet I'll make good on these," James whispered.

Chapter Thirteen

"This is my wife, Summer," James said, his arm around Summer's thick waist. Although she was only six months pregnant, her tummy was full and round. Very round and very full.

"I'm so pleased to meet you."

"Who was that again?" she whispered out of the corner of her mouth.

"Emily Rohrbaugh, the President of the League of Women Voters."

"Oh."

From her small, distressed reaction, James knew Summer found meeting so many people and remembering their names both difficult and distressing.

"I try to tie their name in with something that I'll remember," James told her, willing to share his own method of remembering people's names.

"Rohrbaugh is something of a challenge, don't you think?" Summer returned.

"Roar and baa," he said, under his breath. "Think of a lion and a lamb. Everyone knows a loin roars and a lamb makes a *baa-baa* sound. Rohrbaugh."

Summer's face lit up with a bright smile. "No wonder I married you. You're brilliant."

"I bet you won't have a problem remembering Emily the next time you meet."

"I won't."

"She's a good friend of Elizabeth Manning," James said, and fed his wife a seedless grape. It was a test of his restraint not to kiss her afterward and taste the blend of the grape's and his wife's sweetness. After all these months one would assume his desire for her would fade; if anything, quite the opposite had occurred. She was never more attractive to him than she was now, heavy with their children.

"Elizabeth Manning," Summer repeated. "I didn't think she'd be the political type."

"She isn't," James said. They mingled with the crowd gathered on the patio of an influential member of the state senate. "From what I understand, the two have been friends since high school."

"I see."

"Do you need to sit a spell?"

"James," she groaned. "Stop worrying about me."

He lowered his gaze to her swollen abdomen. "How are Mutt and Jeff?"

She flattened her hand against her side. "I swear these two are going to be world-class soccer players."

James chuckled and reached for an hors d'oeuvre from one of the several platters set around the sunny patio. He hand-fed it to Summer.

"James, I don't believe I've met your wife."

James recognized the voice as belonging to the President of the Bar Association, William Brett. He quickly made the introductions. He never worried about Summer saying the wrong thing or inadvertently doing something that would embarrass him. She had a natural way about her that instantly put people at ease. She was charming and open and genuine. These political functions weren't her cup of tea, but she never complained. She seemed eager to do whatever she could to aid his campaign and had proved to be the asset he knew she would be.

"I'm very pleased to meet you," she said warmly as they exchanged handshakes.

The natural topic of conversation was Summer's pregnancy, which they discussed but only briefly. His wife had a way of deftly turning the conversation away from herself. Soon Brett was talking about himself, laughing over the early days when his wife was pregnant with their oldest child.

After a few minutes Summer excused herself.

"She's an excellent conversationalist," William Brett commented as Summer walked away.

James did his best to hide a smile. It amused him that Brett could do the majority of the talking and then act as if Summer had been the one carrying the discussion.

"It seems strange to think of you as married," the well-known attorney said next.

"When I'm with Summer, I wonder why I ever waited so long."

Brett shifted his weight from one foot to the other. "If I'd given you advice before you were appointed to the court, it would have been to marry."

"Really?" This came as something of a shock to James.

"You're a fine young man, and I expect great things from you. Just between you and me and the fence post, I think you're doing an excellent job."

"I'd like to think so," James said, but such thinking was dangerous. There were some who weren't as confident. Generally those under the influence of Ralph Southworth. What surprised James in the aftermath of their disagreement was that Southworth had managed to prejudice several supporters against him.

"You remind me of myself thirty years back," William Brett told him.

James considered this high praise. "Thank you."

"But you needed a little softening around the edges. You came off as strong and unbending. Not a bad thing for a judge, mind you, but being a tad more human wouldn't have hurt you any, either."

"I see." James didn't like hearing this, but felt it was for his own good, however uncomfortable.

"It's easy to sit in judgment of others when you live in an ivory tower."

James frowned, unsure if he appreciated this conversation. "I don't understand."

"Until you married Summer, your life was sterile and protected. A married man knows what it's like to make compromises. I imagine you've done a thing or two to make your wife happy that you wouldn't normally do."

"True."

"Call me what you will, but in my opinion, marriage matures a man. It helps him sympathize and identify with his fellow humans."

"Are you trying to tell me I was a stodgy stuffed shirt before I married Summer?" James asked outright.

William Brett seemed surprised by his directness, then grinned. "I couldn't have said it better myself."

"That's what I thought." James reached for a cracker topped with cream cheese.

"By the way, I wanted to congratulate you on a job well done. The multiple homicide was your first murder trial, wasn't it?"

James nodded. To be perfectly frank, he was happy it was over. The ordeal had proved to be exhausting for everyone involved. The jury had found the young man guilty, and after careful consideration, James had delivered the sentencing.

James's name and face had appeared on television screens every night for weeks. It went without saying that a lot of people were watching and waiting to see how he'd rule. The liberals were looking for leniency, and the hard-liners wanted the man locked away for the rest of his life. James had agonized over the sentence.

There were more victims than the ones who were shot during those hours of madness. Three families had lost loved ones. Seventeen others carried the mark of a madman's gun. Innocent lives had been forever changed.

James had delivered a sentence that he felt was fair. He didn't look to satisfy any political factions. The outcome of the election could well rest on his judgment.

It would have been impossible to keep everyone happy, and so his decision had been based on what he considered equitable and fair for all concerned. Some were pleased, he knew, and others were outraged.

"Thank you," James said, "I appreciate your vote of confidence."

"The decisions don't get any easier," William Brett told him. The older man reached for a stuffed green olive and popped it in his mouth.

"The bar will be taking their opinion poll about the time your wife's due to deliver those babies of yours."

James knew it was left up to the discretion of the bar whether to publish the results or not. The vote could sway the November election.

Summer returned just then, looking tired. She managed a smile. William Brett seemed to realize this. He wished them his best and drifted away.

"Are you ready to leave?" James asked.

"No," she protested. "We've barely arrived."

"We're going." His mistake was in asking her. He should have known to expect an argument.

James made their excuses, thanked the host and hostess and urged Summer toward their parked car. Her progress was slow, her steps deliberate. He knew she was uncomfortable, especially in the heat.

"Charlotte's due in two weeks," she muttered when he helped her inside the car. She sighed as she eased into the seat. The seat belt would barely stretch all the way around her.

James paused. "What's that comment about Charlotte all about?"

"I envy her. Look at me, James."

"I am looking at you," he said, and planted a kiss on her cheek. "You're the most beautiful woman in the world."

"I don't believe you," she muttered.

"You'd better, because it wouldn't take much to convince me to prove it right here and now."

"James, honestly."

"I am being honest," he insisted.

She smiled, and he couldn't resist kissing her a second time.

After they arrived at the house, Summer sat outside in the warm summer sunshine. She propped her feet on a stool in front of her. Her hands rested on her tummy, which resembled an oversize basketball by this time.

It didn't matter how large she grew with their children; James couldn't look at her and not experience a deep physical ache. He wanted to make love to her, yes, but the ache reached far deeper than some hormonal craving.

James brought her out a glass of iced tea.

She smiled her appreciation. "You spoil me."

"That's because I enjoy it." He sat down next to her. "I don't suppose you've thought about packing up and leaving me lately?"

Summer giggled softly. "Once or twice, but by the time I finished dragging out my suitcases, I was too tired to go."

"You're teasing."

"Of course I'm teasing."

"Speaking of suitcases, do you have one ready for the hospital?"

"Aren't we a little premature?"

"Who knows what Mutt and Jeff are thinking." James's hand joined hers. It thrilled him to feel his children move inside her. "And this time you might want to take more than your toothbrush, a book and your bedroom slippers."

"That goes to show you the mental state I was in."

"Never again," James said in a way so she'd know he wasn't teasing.

Summer propped her head against his shoulder and sighed. "Never again," she agreed.

The day of the September primary, Summer woke feeling sluggish and out of sorts. Getting out of bed was a task of monumental proportion. She felt as if she needed a forklift.

James was already up and shaved. He'd been watching her like a hawk all week. To everyone's surprise, including her doctor's, Summer hadn't delivered the twins. She'd read that twins were often born early. But not Mutt and Jeff, the affectionate names James had dubbed their children.

"Babies aren't born on their due date, so stop looking so worried. This is your important day." She sat on the edge of the mattress and pressed her hand to the small of her back.

James offered her his arm to help her upright. "How do you feel?"

"I don't know yet." The pain in the base of her spine had kept her awake most of the night. It didn't seem to want to go away, no matter what she did.

"When are we voting?" she asked.

"First thing this morning," James told her.

"Good."

"Why is that good?" he asked anxiously. "Do you think today's the day?"

"James, stop, I'm in perfect health."

"For someone nine months pregnant with twins, you mean."

Summer swore that somehow, God willing, she'd make it through this day. James was so tender and endearing, but she didn't want him worrying about her on the day of the primary election.

They gathered with Walter at the large Manning family home for the election results that evening. Summer was pleased for the opportunity to be with her friends.

Jason and Charlotte, along with their toddler and infant daughter, Ann Marie, were the first to arrive.

Many of the friends who'd worked so hard on James's campaign showed up shortly before the first election results were announced.

Summer planted herself in a chair in the family room and didn't move. The ache in her back had intensified, and she tried to rub it.

Feeling the need to stand up and move about, Summer made her way into the kitchen. She was in front of the sink when it happened. Her eyes rounded as she felt a sharp, stabbing pain.

"James," she cried in a panic, and gripped hold of the counter. Water gushed from between her legs and onto the floor. "Oh, my goodness."

"Summer?" James stood in the doorway, along with at least ten others, including Elizabeth Manning.

"I'm sorry," she whispered, looking to James. "But I think it might be time to take me to the hospital."

She saw her husband turn and stare longingly at the election result being flashed across the television screen. "Now?"

Chapter Fourteen

"James...I'm sorry." The pain that had been concentrated in the small of her back worked its way around her middle. Summer held her tummy and closed her eyes, surprised by the intensity of it.

"Sorry," James demanded, "for what?" He joined her and placed his arm around her shoulder.

"You'd best get her to the hospital," Elizabeth advised.

"I'll phone the doctor for you," Eric insisted.

James shouted out the memorized number, and five or six of the Mannings chanted it until Eric found a pen and pad with which to write it down.

Summer felt as if all at once everyone wanted to play a role in the birth of their twins.

"Toss me the car keys, and I'll get the car as close to the front door as I can," Jason Manning told her husband.

James threw his friend the car keys, and Jason hurried out the front door.

"What about the election returns?" Summer asked, gazing longingly toward the television.

"I'll find out about them later," James insisted as if it meant nothing.

"I'll phone the results into the hospital every hour," Charlotte volunteered, "and James can give us an update on Summer and the babies."

Summer bit into her lower lip at the approach of another contraction. It hurt, really hurt. "James." She squeezed his hand, needing him.

"I'm here, sweetheart. I won't leave you, not for anything."

Jason reappeared, and the small entourage headed for James's car. It was parked on the grass, close to the front door, the engine running.

"The doctor said you should go directly to the hospital," Walter called out breathlessly. "He'll meet you there."

"Don't worry, Summer, this isn't his first set of twins," Elizabeth said reassuringly.

"True, but they're mine," James said.

"James?" Summer looked at her husband and noticed for the first time how pale he'd become. "Are you all right?"

He didn't answer her for a moment; instead, he helped ease her inside the car and lovingly strapped her in with the seat belt. Before long he sat next to her, his hand braced against the steering wheel. Summer noticed his pulse pounding in the vein in his neck.

"It's going to be fine," she reassured him.

"I'll feel a whole lot better once we get you to the hospital."

"Call us," Charlotte shouted, standing on the front steps and waving.

Summer waved back, and no less than ten or fifteen adults crowded onto the Mannings' front steps waving and cheering them on.

"James, are you all right to drive?" Summer asked when he took off at breakneck speed. He stayed within the speed limit, but there was a leashed fear in him that was almost palpable.

"I'll be all right once we get you to the hospital and under medical care."

"The birthing process is all perfectly natural."

"Maybe it is for a woman, but it isn't as easy as it looks for a man."

With her hands propped against her abdomen, Summer smiled. "What's that supposed to mean?"

"I don't know that I can bear to see you in terrible pain," he said, and wiped a hand down his face when they stopped for a red light.

"It's not so bad."

"Thus far, you mean. You saw the films with me at the birthing class. I don't know if I'm ready for this."

"You!" she said, and giggled.

James's fingers curled around her hand. "This isn't a laughing matter. I don't know that I've ever been more frightened in my life. Once," he amended, and his gaze briefly left hers. "The night I came home and found you gone."

"The babies and I are going to be just fine. Don't worry, darling, please. This is your night to shine. My one regret is that Mutt and Jeff chose now to make their debut."

"Right now the election is the last thing on my mind. None of it matters."

"You're going to win the primary," she insisted. Summer knew the competition had been steep, and Ralph Southworth had done what damage he could, eager to prove himself right.

"We're almost to the hospital," James said, and he sounded relieved.

"Relax," she said, and as it turned out, her words were a reminder to herself. The contraction hit with unexpected severity, and she drew in a deep breath in an effort to control the pain.

"Summer."

"I'm fine," she said, doing her best to hide how severe the pain was.

James pulled into the emergency entrance at Virginia Mason Hospital and raced around the front of the vehicle. He opened the door, unsnapped the seat belt and lovingly helped her out of the car.

Someone rolled a wheelchair her way, and while Summer sat and answered the brief questions in admitting, James parked the car.

She was on the maternity floor when he rejoined her. The first thing she noticed when he walked into the room was how terribly pale and harried he looked.

"Stop worrying," she told him.

James scooted a chair to the side of her bed and slumped into it. "Feel my heart," he said, and pressed her hand over his hard chest.

"It feels like a machine gun," Summer said, and smiled. She moved her hand to his face and cupped his cheek.

"I need you so much," James whispered.

Summer couldn't answer due to a strong contraction. James gripped her hand in his and talked to her in soothing tones, urging her to relax. As the pain ebbed away, she kept her eyes closed.

When she opened them again, she found James standing by the hospital bed, studying her. She smiled weakly, and he returned the gesture.

Dr. Wise arrived and read her chart, then asked, "How are we doing here?"

"Great," Summer assured him.

"Not so good," James contradicted. "Summer needs something for the pain, and frankly I'm not feeling so well myself."

"James, I'm fine," Summer told him.

"What your husband's saying is that he needs something to help him deal with seeing you in pain," the physician explained.

"Do something, Doc."

Dr. Wise affectionately slapped James across the back. "Why don't we let Summer be the one to decide when she needs the painkiller? She's a better judge of when she'll need something than either one of us."

"All right." But James's agreement came reluctantly.

The hours passed for Summer in a blur. Her labor proved to be difficult, and she was sure she never could have endured it if not for James, who stood faithfully at her side. He encouraged her, lifted her spirits, rubbed her back, reassured her of his love.

News of the primary filtered into the labor room. In the beginning Summer strained to hear each bit of information on James's bid for the seat on the superior court. But as the evening wore on, she became so involved in what was happening to her and the babies that she barely heard.

Summer lost track of time, but it seemed to her it was well into the wee hours of the morning when she was taken into the delivery room.

James briefly left her side and returned a few moments later gowned in a surgical green outfit. He resembled a prison escapee, and she took one look at him and giggled.

"What's so funny?" he enquired.

"You."

James drew in a deep breath and held on to Summer's hand. "It's almost time."

"I know," she breathed softly. "Ready or not, we're about to become parents. I have the feeling this is going to be the ride of a lifetime."

"It's been that way for me from the time I first met you."

"Are you sorry, James?"

"Sorry?" he repeated, and laughed softly. Leaning over, he kissed her forehead. "My only regret is that I didn't marry you that first year."

"Oh, James, I do love you so."

Dr. Wise joined them. "Well, you two, let's see what we've got here, shall we?"

Two months later Summer woke to the soft, mewling cry of her infant daughter. So as not to disrupt James, she silently climbed out of bed and made her way into their daughters' nursery.

There she found James sitting upright in the rocker, sound asleep with Kellie in his arms. Kerrie fussed from the crib.

Lifting the tiny bundle from the crib, Summer changed the infant's diaper and then sat down in the rocker next to her husband and bared her breast to her hungry child. Kerrie nursed eagerly, and Summer ran her finger down the side of her baby's perfect pink face.

Her gaze wandered to her husband, and she felt a surge of pride and love for him. The election was over now, and he'd won the court seat by a wide margin. During the heat of the past two weeks of the campaign, James had let her compose and sing a radio commercial for him. Summer had been proud of her small part in his success. She didn't miss life on the stage. Her identical twin daughters kept her far too busy for regrets.

James must have felt her scrutiny because he stirred. He looked up and noticed Summer with Kerrie.

"I might as well feed Kellie, too," she suggested. Experience had taught her that the minute one was fed and down, and Summer returned to bed, the other twin would wake and demand to be nursed. It amazed her how identical her twin daughters were. Even their sleep patterns were the same.

James stood and expertly changed Kellie's diaper.

When Kerrie finished nursing, Summer swapped babies with him. James gently placed his daughter on his shoulder and patted her back until they heard the tiny burp.

"Why didn't you wake me?" Summer asked.

"You were sleeping so soundly."

"It was quite a night, Your Honor," she said, looking over at her husband. "I couldn't be more proud of you, James. Your position on the court is secure now."

"I couldn't have done it without you," he told her.

"Don't be ridiculous."

"It's true," he whispered with feeling. "You and Kerrie and Kellie. The voters fell in love with the three of you. Those radio commercials you sang were the talk of the town. I'm the envy of every politician I know."

"Because I can sing?"

"No, because you're my wife." His eyes were dark and intense. "I'm crazy about you, Summer. I still can't believe all you've given me."

"I love you, too, James." Summer closed her eyes and relaxed. It had started all those months ago in Vegas when it felt as if her heart were breaking. Now her heart was filled to overflowing. Life couldn't get any better than what it was right then, she decided.

But Summer was wrong.

The very best had yet to come.

* * * * *

Get Ready to be Swept Away by
Silhouette's Spring Collection

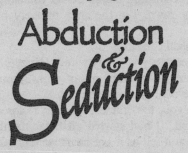

Abduction
& Seduction

These passion-filled stories explore both the dangerous
desires of men and the seductive powers of women.
Written by three of our most celebrated authors, they are
sure to capture your hearts.

Diana Palmer
Brings us a spin-off of her Long, Tall Texans series

Joan Johnston
Crafts a beguiling Western romance

Rebecca Brandewyne
New York Times bestselling author
makes a smashing contemporary debut

Available in March at your favorite retail outlet.

MILLION DOLLAR SWEEPSTAKES (III)

No purchase necessary. To enter, follow the directions published. Method of entry may vary. For eligibility, entries must be received no later than March 31, 1996. No liability is assumed for printing errors, lost, late or misdirected entries. Odds of winning are determined by the number of eligible entries distributed and received. Prizewinners will be determined no later than June 30, 1996.

Sweepstakes open to residents of the U.S. (except Puerto Rico), Canada, Europe and Taiwan who are 18 years of age or older. All applicable laws and regulations apply. Sweepstakes offer void wherever prohibited by law. Values of all prizes are in U.S. currency. This sweepstakes is presented by Torstar Corp., its subsidiaries and affiliates, in conjunction with book, merchandise and/or product offerings. For a copy of the Official Rules send a self-addressed, stamped envelope (WA residents need not affix return postage) to: MILLION DOLLAR SWEEPSTAKES (III) Rules, P.O. Box 4573, Blair, NE 68009, USA.

EXTRA BONUS PRIZE DRAWING

No purchase necessary. The Extra Bonus Prize will be awarded in a random drawing to be conducted no later than 5/30/96 from among all entries received. To qualify, entries must be received by 3/31/96 and comply with published directions. Drawing open to residents of the U.S. (except Puerto Rico), Canada, Europe and Taiwan who are 18 years of age or older. All applicable laws and regulations apply; offer void wherever prohibited by law. Odds of winning are dependent upon number of eligibile entries received. Prize is valued in U.S. currency. The offer is presented by Torstar Corp., its subsidiaries and affiliates in conjunction with book, merchandise and/or product offering. For a copy of the Official Rules governing this sweepstakes, send a self-addressed, stamped envelope (WA residents need not affix return postage) to: Extra Bonus Prize Drawing Rules, P.O. Box 4590, Blair, NE 68009, USA.

SWP-S295

Over 12 million books in print!

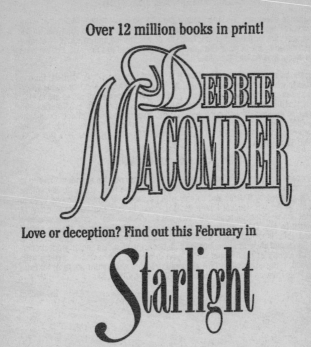

DEBBIE MACOMBER

Love or deception? Find out this February in

Starlight

Rand Prescott is a man who stubbornly refuses to open his heart. Karen McAlister is a woman who has to prove that her vows were said in love and not deception. Now she must try everything to convince Rand that they were meant to be together—forever.

When wedding vows aren't enough...

THE SULTAN'S WIVES
Tracy Sinclair
(SE #943, March)

When a story in an exotic locale beckoned, nothing could keep Pippa Bennington from scooping the competition. But this time, her eager journalist's heart landed her squarely in, of all things, a harem! Pippa was falling for the seductive charms of Mikolar al-Rasheed—but what exactly *were* the sultan's true intentions?

Don't miss
THE SULTAN'S WIVES,
by Tracy Sinclair,
available in March!

She's friend, wife, mother—she's you! And beside each Special Woman stands a wonderfully *special* man. It's a celebration of our heroines— and the men who become part of their lives.

Silhouette

SPECIAL EDITION™

WHAT EVER HAPPENED TO...?

Have you been wondering when much-loved characters will finally get their own stories? Well, have we got a lineup for you! Silhouette Special Edition is proud to present a *Spin-off Spectacular!* Be sure to catch these exciting titles from some of your favorite authors:

HUSBAND: SOME ASSEMBLY REQUIRED (SE #931 January) Shawna Saunders has finally found Mr. Right in the dashing Murphy Pendleton, last seen in *Marie Ferrarella*'s BABY IN THE MIDDLE (SE #892).

SAME TIME, NEXT YEAR (SE #937 February) In this tie-in to *Debbie Macomber*'s popular series THOSE MANNING MEN and THOSE MANNING SISTERS, a yearly reunion between friends suddenly has them in the marrying mood!

A FAMILY HOME (SE #938 February) Adam Cutler discovers the best reason for staying home is the love he's found with sweet-natured and sexy Lainey Bates in *Celeste Hamilton*'s follow-up to WHICH WAY IS HOME? (SE #897).

JAKE'S MOUNTAIN (SE #945 March) Jake Harris never met anyone as stubborn—or as alluring—as Dr. Maggie Matthews in *Christine Flynn*'s latest, a spin-off to WHEN MORNING COMES (SE #922).

Don't miss these wonderful titles, only for our readers—only from Silhouette Special Edition!

If you are looking for more titles by

DEBBIE MACOMBER,

don't miss these heartwarming stories by one of
Silhouette's most popular authors:

Silhouette Special Edition®

#09756	BRIDE ON THE LOOSE+	$3.39	☐
#09798	HASTY WEDDING	$3.39	☐
#09831	GROOM WANTED*	$3.50	☐
#09836	BRIDE WANTED*	$3.50	☐
#09842	MARRIAGE WANTED*	$3.50	☐

+Those Manning Men
*From This Day Forward

Men Made in America

#45152	BORROWED DREAMS	$3.59	☐

TOTAL AMOUNT	$
POSTAGE & HANDLING ($1.00 for one book, 50¢ for each additional)	$
APPLICABLE TAXES*	$_____
TOTAL PAYABLE (check or money order—please do not send cash)	$_____

To order, complete this form and send it, along with a check or money order
for the total above, payable to Silhouette Books, to: **In the U.S.:** 3010 Walden
Avenue, P.O. Box 9047, Buffalo, NY 14269-9047; **In Canada:** P.O. Box 636,
Fort Erie, Ontario, L2A 5X3.

Name:_____

Address:_____ City:_____

State/Prov.:_____ Zip/Postal Code:_____

*New York residents remit applicable sales taxes.
Canadian residents remit applicable GST and provincial taxes.   SDMBACK5

Silhouette®
™